1 MONTH OF
FREE
READING

at

www.ForgottenBooks.com

By purchasing this book you are eligible for one month membership to ForgottenBooks.com, giving you unlimited access to our entire collection of over 1,000,000 titles via our web site and mobile apps.

To claim your free month visit:

www.forgottenbooks.com/free5569

ISBN 978-0-483-39003-4
PIBN 10005569

This book is a reproduction of an important historical work. Forgotten Books uses state-of-the-art technology to digitally reconstruct the work, preserving the original format whilst repairing imperfections present in the aged copy. In rare cases, an imperfection in the original, such as a blemish or missing page, may be replicated in our edition. We do, however, repair the vast majority of imperfections successfully; any imperfections that remain are intentionally left to preserve the state of such historical works.

JANE HUDSON.

JANE HUDSON,

THE AMERICAN GIRL;

.

OR,

EXERT YOURSELF.

.

LONDON:

THE RELIGIOUS TRACT SOCIETY;

Instituted 1799.

DEPOSITORY, 56, PATERNOSTER ROW, AND 65, ST. PAUL'S CHURCHYARD; AND SOLD BY THE BOOKSELLERS.

LONDON:

THE RELIGIOUS TRACT SOCIETY;

PREFACE

THE ENGLISH EDITION.

THIS lively and useful narrative was written for the young people of the United States of America. It contains several references to customs and manners which differ from those of England; but these appear suited to enforce the important lesson of the book—the duty of exerting ourselves in fulfilling the duties of life. This work also shows that " godliness is profitable unto all things, having promise of the life that now is, and of that which is to come."—1 TIM. iv. 8.

CONTENTS.

JANE HUDSON.

A PATCH.

"'Have you put your clean clothes away, Jane?"

" Yes, mother, as nicely as can be, and nothing wanted mending."

" Well, now you may take off your plaid frock, and sit down and try to patch the elbow," said she.

" Oh, mother, not now," I said, in a very beseeching tone. " I have such a beautiful book to read, Cornelia Gordon lent me! She said she never stirred till she finished it. It is a wonder the baby was left to her care; but she let him cry in the cradle, till he cried it out. It is beautiful, mother!" and I pressed the book to my bosom.

" Go and change your dress, my dear," repeated my mother.

" Oh, it is so pleasant! and pleasant Wednesday afternoons do not often come," said I, pushing up the window, and observing the state of the weather. " I do not want to patch; I would rather walk, mother."

B

" I dare say you would, Jane, but I should think you would be quite ashamed of your elbow."

" I am sorry, mother. I should like to put on my best dress, but I do not like patching this now;" and I opened the delightful book.

" Is that minding mother, Jane?" asked Jemmy, who was making a ball in the chimney corner.

I began to read.

" Will you come here, Jane?"

As I approached her, she took my hand, and with her black eyes looking full and meaningly into mine, she said, " Remember this, my daughter: never suffer yourself to indulge in any pleasure, either with a book, or by a walk, or otherwise, to the neglect of a single household duty. If you do, you will find yourself among that great company of women, who go through this life with holes in both elbows."

I cast down my eyes, then looked sidewise towards Jemmy, and saw that his were fixed inquiringly upon my mother's face.

" Who are they, mother?" he at length asked. " I never saw them."

" Nor I. I am sure I do not want to keep company with those who cannot mend their elbows," trying to withdraw my hand.

" I am afraid you will, Jane," she said seriously, still looking closely at me.

" I hope not," said Jemmy.

" I *will not!*" exclaimed I, reddening. " Where do they stay?"

" They are women, who are willing to attend to everything else before their home duties.

Yet home duties, Jane, are a woman's peculiar duties. If she neglect them, they will never be done at all. A woman may be very learned, very intelligent, very agreeable; but still, if she does not or will not attend to the sweeping, cleaning, darning, mending, etc., of her own family, she is as sadly out of the way, as glaringly deficient in all that would make her a truly complete and useful woman, as if she were dressed ever so richly, yet with holes in her elbows."

" I think everybody would pity her for the holes more than they would admire her dress, mother," cried Jemmy.

" Everybody would see them and call her a foolish woman, mother! not to know how to take care of her elbows!" said I.

" She would certainly be considered as lacking some important qualification. So you think, upon the whole, Jane, you would not wish to join such a company?" still looking straight at me.

" No, indeed, mother, I hope not!"

" Then you must see to it, now, while you are a child, that the common household duties which belong to you are faithfully discharged. The common household duties are those which most easily escape us, though they are those upon which our comforts mainly depend. Faithfully finish these first, Jane; then take your leisure for reading, walking, or whatever pleasant recreation is proper."

" I understand it all, mother," said I, as she paused, " and I will off with my plaid this minute and mend it," thankful to see a way open to get my hand released, and to hide my face from her penetrating glance.

Behold, then, the child, not long after, seated by a table, with needle, scissors, patch, and instructions how to proceed, casting now a glance out at the window, now at the book, then settling down upon the well-worn plaid in her lap. There was a business-like air about her, notwithstanding stray desires lurking within her heart, that were quite unbusiness-like.

" After you have finished, you can go out if you wish. Jemmy and Mary can take care of themselves," said my mother, on re-entering the room, dressed in a plain suit of mourning, and intent upon an errand into the village.

" Oh, mother, before you go, take Jane's book and put it away. She will steal into it; it will be a temptation she cannot stand, I know," looking at me all the time.

" Perhaps it is best to try her, Jemmy," answered she. " If Jane cannot withstand temptations, she is not worth anything; she will be like the leaf, turning with every wind that blows. While she is young, she must strengthen herself. A woman's life is made up of little doings, so small that they sometimes seem of little consequence, and she is easily tempted to set them aside or put them off to a more convenient season; yet, little as they are, they are links in a long chain of duty; and as the loss of one link separates the chain, so one duty out of season disorders a whole day. Let Jane sit in the very face of the book and the weather, and courage-

ously sew on the patch in spite of them. She
will be a stronger and a better girl for it."

" Oh, I see it!" exclaimed I, my imagination
seizing upon the chain. " If I do not patch
now, when will it be patched? That is the
question. If I put it off till night, then I cannot learn my lesson; if I do not learn my lesson
to-night, why, I must learn it to-morrow; if to-
morrow, I may be late at school. I see it, mother," I said, heartily. " I see it! This is the
link, now, to make the chain whole for a good
many days to come, perhaps!" And I earnestly
twitched the patch this way and that, to make
it match the stripes. Seeing things in so hopeful a train, she departed. Nor had she been
gone long, before a group of girls ran up the
step and knocked.

" Come, oh, come, Jane; we want you to go
to walk!" they exclaimed. " It is a fine day!
Put your things on quickly!" and they all
huddled in.

" I cannot," I said, " I must finish my work
first!"

" Do you mean that patching?" asked Cornelia. "You patching! A girl patch!" exclaimed
a second and third. " I am sure I would not
stay in and patch such a day as this, if I never
had anything patched!"

" Then you will be likely to be a person out
at both elbows," said Jemmy, peeping through
Susan White's curls. Susan had thrown off her
hood, and cast herself among his playthings.

" _I_ out at both elbows!" exclaimed Cornelia,
tossing back her head. " _I_ can always have my
mending done _for_ me! _I_ do not mend!"

"Those are just the ones," persisted Jemmy.

"I do not know how to mend. My father is rich enough without my mending," and she stalked to and fro, like a little queen.

"Some time or other you will see whether you are not out at both elbows," reiterated Jemmy. Cornelia reddened with anger, and looked at me.

"Oh, it is only some of Jim's fun," said I, "do not mind him. There he sits, in the corner, and says just what he pleases, and we always let him, because he is ill."

"Are you not going? I am," she said, not relishing Jemmy's fun, in spite of my apology.

"I cannot possibly go now! I must stick to my patch until it is in!" not daring to look out at the window, for fear of being tempted.

"It is too bad for your mother to make you work so!" said Cornelia. "Come, girls, let us go! I wish you would go, Jane; it is too pleasant to work! I declare it is! I would throw the patch into the fire, and run away!"

"I have a great mind to do so," I said, laughing. Jemmy looked reprovingly up.

"Oh, have you read this book, Jane?" said she, espying it on the table.

"My patch! This comes first; house duties before books, mother says!"

"Your patch!" she echoed, provokingly. "Your patch! I think your mother is hard on you, Jane; why, mine would not think of asking me to do any such thing. She lets me do as I have a mind to do about such things."

Something like wishing for just such an easy time as Cornelia had, was on my lips. It was not the first, neither was it the last time. I surveyed her, beautifully dressed in her chinchilla hat, and new Caroline plaid pelisse, and Angola gloves, and thought—"She will never have to patch, not she! I am likely to patch all the days of my life, beginning so early!"

Ah, I understand how to reason better now! And then, as I surveyed her again, how I wished to be as lucky as some little orphans I had read about, who found the pot of gold coins; or if a fairy would only grant me three wishes, or—— then could I be like Cornelia, have what I desired, and read when I was in the mood to read, and do anything I wished. Yes! and never touch a patch! So I thought, as the girls hopped and skipped after her into the street, I following them to the door with longing eyes, on that bright Wednesday afternoon.

"It does seem almost too bad, does it not, Jemmy, that I cannot go, but must be tied up here to my old elbow, such a pleasant day as this is?"

"I believe mother is right about it, though," answered James. "Mother is always found at last to be right, you know, though it does not always seem as if she would."

"But do you not think it is sometimes very hard?" asked I.

"It is our duty to do it, mother says."

It was not exactly what I wished him to say. I wanted more sympathy or pity, but Jemmy always sturdily arrayed himself on the side of "mother says."

Distastefully turning towards the patch, I cast side glances at the book.

"One peep in the book—just one! To see how it reads. Only a minute. A minute is not much. I hate patching!" So tempting fancies went and came, almost carrying me away in their current.

"No! No! No!" was the sober second thought—hard in coming, but firm when it did come. "No! No! No! Mother let the book stay there to try me, and shall it be said that I had not courage enough to resist it? No! I will not be so weak as all that comes to. I will let her know I can be trusted! Common duties first. Our comforts depend on these, mother says, and these depend on us women. No! I will never have holes at both elbows! never!" And away flew my needle, to stop, in time, every opening to so unfavourable an issue. Stitch! stitch! stitch! There I sat, with all the dignity and industry of thirty, instead of ten.

In due time the patch was on—well on—"nicely on;"—so mother pronounced it to be, on careful examination.

Thus much for my first patch.

FIRST EARNINGS.

I was not long in comprehending that our circumstances were greatly changed by our father's death, and that I, as the eldest child, must begin to take my share in housekeeping at present, as well as look forward towards taking care of myself for the future. My mother was neither complaining nor despairing, but with

cheerful energy she did her best, with all the
means she could bring together. By sewing,
she contrived to eke out our scanty resource,
while the house, (a small tenement,) a narrow
piece of land, and a cow, were our main support. During the winter, when not attending
school, I used to sit and sew with her, and
though with little variety in our meals, and less
in our occupation, save in

> " Seam, gusset and band,
>   And band, gusset and seam,"

a more contented, cheerful family could not have
been found, than mother and her four little
ones. Sometimes helping her on with her work,
sometimes beguiling her with Pilgrim's Progress, or the Listener, or the Gleaner, or hearken-
ing to her pleasant stories, we were very happy
children.

By and by, it seemed to me as if I must be
earning something myself.

"What could I do?" was a perplexing and
momentous question, considered and reconsi-
dered every night and morning. "What could
be done?" "What?" At length a lucky
thought struck me. Annual "cattle-shows"
were held in the village in those days—long
since, I believe, changed in name, or discon-
tinned, or transferred to other places. Besides
varieties of remarkable cattle, present upon such
occasions, (including most four-footed beasts, if
not creeping things,) the farmers' wives and
daughters brought all sorts of specimens of
household skill, such as yarn, stockings, cloth,
carpets, sufficient to fill a large hall; a small

premium, or prize, being usually awarded to these, for the purpose of encouraging home manufactures. Working muslin was in fashion then, and, being already skilful in this species of needlework, I asked if I could not work a cape for the "cattle-show," especially as I had a small muslin cape cut out, ready to be wrought.

"I can do it, I know I can!" blowing the embers furiously at the thought, being engaged at that moment in kindling a fire under the tea-kettle, for breakfast. "I can get up earlier, and take time away from play. Yes! I will do it, and do all my other duties too; and I will do it, and not let mother know it till it is done, fairly finished!"

The thought of pleasing her, and of aiding her too, animated me all the forenoon. In the evening, taking the roll of patterns from her basket, I asked which was a pretty one for my cape. She looked them over and decided upon one, which I immediately selected; nor did she in the least suspect my design. The plan was soon in successful operation, my only fear being that it might not be completed in time. The first few sprigs went rapidly on. As the weather grew colder, (some time, I think, in October,) I well remember how I used to shrink from leaving my snug quarters in bed, to accomplish my morning work.

"A minute more! only a minute!" I begged of myself, after popping up my head enough to feel the autumn chill.

"Oh, no!" I said to myself, creeping up, "this will not do, it will not! I must persevere, in spite of wind or weather, warm beds or

short naps! I must carry on what I undertake!
I must be business-like! I must!"—and out I
sprang from my warm nest, on the small strip
of carpet that lay by the bed-side.

Even a few stitches were so much gained.
Indeed, my cape actually grew, little by little,
leaf by leaf, sprig by sprig.

One pleasant noon, when every moment was
precious, the cattle-show drawing on apace, I
took my lap-bag—a convenient article worn by
girls in those days—and went out into the back
part of our small barn, where a door opened
into a neighbouring field. Here I had often
gone to be by myself, when a hard lesson
was on my hands; sitting for the half hour
together, in summer weather, in that back barn-
door, with the green grass before my eyes, the
soft air blowing through the barn, and wisps of
straw astir here and there, I am afraid I used
to muse as much as I studied, and perhaps a
little more; for children enjoy a great deal in
the quiet indulgence of their fancies, strange
and fantastic though they be. Now I went out
to sew.

It was a warm autumn day, and everything
wore the beautiful and animated hue of that
season. I looked long around, out of the back
barn-door, and the more I looked the more I
longed to throw down my work, and run about!
Happy voices and loud hallooing were heard in
the distance; the crickets were merry as they
could be; the trees and blue sky seemed to

beckon to me to come out. My old disposition
to hate work came violently upon me. Old
habits of lingering and lolling in pleasant paths
began to annoy me.

" I will give up the cape! What is the use?
I am not going to sit here and sew! I cannot
get it done! What is the use of trying? And
then, perhaps, I shall get nothing for my pains!
It is a great deal pleasanter to go out some-
where, and enjoy myself. I do not want to
sew! I hate to sew!"

I felt that I was sorely tempted! tempted!
tempted! Then, dropping my hands before my
eyes, I said aloud, as if to re-assure my waning
energies by something addressed to the ear:

" I must carry on what I undertake! I must
do my best! I must! I must go through! If
I ever wish to be anything, I must not lag by
the way, mother says. I cannot get the cape
done, did I say? I can get it done, and I will!"
The struggle was severe, and lasted for some
time. It was a hard battle, and for hours the
victory seemed doubtful.

Such is one of the eras in every child's life,
which make or unmake him. It is the result of
the inward conflict which decides the future
character. Under the parental eye or the chastening rod, a child may feel constrained to decide right. The grand aim of moral training is
only secured when he can be made to decide
right FROM PRINCIPLE, in the hundred temptations which are encountered away from such
influences, when he is alone, by himself.

The conviction that the eye of God is upon
our thoughts as well as upon our ways; that

there is a law which He has revealed; that it is holy, just, and good; and that we are bound, by its eternal sanctions, to obey it, must have firm hold upon the mind even of a child, or the issue of such struggles is likely to be disastrous. One that honours his father and his mother, in the fear of God, and in obedience to His precepts, will refrain from any act which he believes they would disapprove, as carefully in their absence as in their presence. No lower motive, no less controlling principle, will secure him from ·falling into temptations and snares. Whatever I thought then, these are my sober thoughts now.

The scale turned, and on the right side. " I can, and will at least try! Mother says, Try! TRY can do wonders. Try, then, hands!" And hands, then properly set to work, under proper authority, did try. There I sat, bending over the muslin, until the sprig allotted for the noon's work was finished. I had parcelled it out, in order to be sure of completing it in a given time.

One Saturday evening, a few days before the cattle-show, I brought the cape, and laid it on my mother's knee, only a few nice finishing strokes being needed.

" Your cape, Jane! Is it possible?" she exclaimed, amazed.

" My cape, mother! I worked it for the cattle-show; perhaps they will give me something for it, as they give other people for theirs. I want to earn something for you, mother!"

How well do I remember the expression of wonderful and earnest interest with which she

C

turned around and looked into my face, as it half rested upon her shoulder. Then she examined it carefully, and asked me when I did it.

"At odd times—moments I stole. And now do you think, after all my pains, I shall get anything for it? I want to get something to help you with!"

"It is of little consequence whether you get anything or not."

A sense of keen disappointment came over me. "She does not think it worth anything," thought I.

"Of comparatively little consequence," she continued, "when you consider the great benefit you have yourself obtained by making and persevering in this effort. Your prospect for becoming a firmer and more useful woman, if your life is spared, was never so hopeful as it is at this moment. You are more of a girl than I thought you were, Jane," and she kissed my forehead.

The next week, she placed some stitches here and there, improved it with her scissors, and pressed it out with a flat iron. "Really," she said, holding it up, "it is quite a cape!"

"A beauty! I think, mother," exclaimed George, trying to lay hold of it with fingers whose last contact had been with the heap of potatoes.

My mother suffered the whole business to go into my hands. She directed me how to write my name and age, and pin the label on; then gave me a little box to fold it up in, and sent me to take it to a gentleman, who must decide if it had sufficient merit for a place in the hall, and, if so, to ask him to make the proper disposition of it.

It was my first business transaction, and I wonder how my heart was kept from leaping out of my mouth, timid child as I was, when, with trembling hand, I knocked at his door, early one morning.

The knock was answered, and I inquired for Mr. Hale.

" He is at breakfast."

The sharp, quick tones of the servant girl frightened me, as she stood staring, neither offering to call Mr. Hale, nor asking me in. Plucking up courage, I begged if she would just ask him to step to the door a minute. It seemed as if I stood there a very, very long time.

By and by, a heavy tread resounded along the entry, and behold Mr. Hale, tall, portly-looking Mr. Hale, appeared before me. Was he ever so tall before?

I in vain tried to speak as he approached me.

" Good morning, little girl! You are out early."

Reassured by his kind manner, I reached out my purple hand with the box containing my treasure. " Will you please put this, sir, in the cattle-show ?" I faintly said.

" The cattle-show ! Ah ! something for the cattle-show, is it, eh ! Well, is it your work?"

" Yes, sir."

" And what is your name ?" He took the box and opened it. " Why, you are quite a little woman to work for the cattle-show. Your name ?" and he bent down towards me.

" Jane Hudson, sir."

" Jane! Jane Hudson! Ah, yes. I know
your good mother. And so you have done
something for the cattle-show, have you, Jane?
Yes, my dear, I will see to it. I am glad to
have some specimens of our village manufac-
ture."

Tears of delight filled my eyes, as I tried to
say, " Thank you, sir," and then hastened home-
wards with a skip and a jump which, under
any other circumstances, might have been quite
boisterous.

" He is going to put it in, Mr. Hale is! He
says he is glad I did it!" I cried, bursting
into the kitchen. Puss retired under the table,
while Mary and Jemmy shrank away from two
or three strange antics, which I unwittingly
made.

The morning which ushered Thursday in
was a very important day to me. I awoke at
break of day, and shook Mary to inform her
that the weather promised to be fair and pleasant.

———

In the forenoon, the hall was to be open for
exhibition, and people were passing in, around
and out, all the day, to examine the various
articles. Mother dressed Mary and myself
neatly, and gave us permission to go likewise.
I now think there must have been a greatly
excited manner about me, as I tripped along;
for, somehow, I expected the first thing to behold, on entering, a wrought cape, hanging at
some conspicuous corner, and attracting general

observation; nor is it peculiar to childhood alone, to imagine that the little things which fill our own hearts, must interest the minds and fill the eyes of everybody else.

On entering, I involuntarily stared around, over people's heads and under their arms; but no cape was to be seen! There were piles upon piles of cloth, and a mass of all sorts of things, for use and ornament.

Choked and jammed, and at the risk of losing my little sister a dozen times, we made our way around the hall, for we seemed always to be where the greatest number were present. I now remember that the sides of the hall were lined with articles. I do not recollect any of them, but I do recollect not to have seen the cape! Once we thought we espied it; but no sooner was the supposed happy discovery made, than we were rudely jostled from our post of observation, and could not regain it.

Ten days afterwards, Mr. Hale called at the door, Mr. Hale himself, and asked for my mother. Mary told him she was away. I ran into the entry at the sound of his voice.

"Ah, there is Jane!" he said, pleasantly. "There she is," putting his hand in his pocket. "Here is your pretty cape, and here is a premium for it," handing me a five shilling piece.

I could not believe my own eyes! A whole crown! Five shillings!

"Five shillings, Jemmy!" I shrieked, running back into the kitchen. "Five shillings for my cape, and my cape besides!" Jemmy took the money, and turned it over and over in his thin fingers, with wondering eyes.

"It is a crown, Jane," he slowly uttered, "a real silver crown!"

"Here, mother! here are five shillings for you!" I ran out at the door to meet her, holding up the money before her face. Mr. Hale just brought it to me for my cape, mother!" I was a thankful, happy creature that day.

For many days, I fancied it was the easiest thing in the world to earn money; forgetting, in the glad possession of my dollar, all the toil. It was a fancy easily dissipated, as everybody knows who has tried it.

My success in this matter of the cape was useful to me. I then felt the truth of the wise man's saying, that the hand of the diligent maketh rich. I now feel that the same earnestness of purpose and the same intentness of pursuit might then have secured me (with the Divine blessing) treasures in Heaven that are imperishable.

———

THE GREEN LANE SCHOOL.

QUITE early in life, and by a kind of common consent, I seemed to be destined to push my fortunes as a teacher.

"Study hard, Jane," (my mother used to say,) "you will find a use for all the knowledge you can get. Up and be doing, Jane! What is truly valuable can only be gained by labour!"

"Oh, mother!" I said once, when she bade me fill the tea-kettle for tea, "I wish I was as well off as Cornelia Gordon! She has such easy times! She never does anything unless she has a mind to do it!"

"I pity Cornelia," answered she, spiritedly, "from my heart. She will, I am afraid, dream away half her life. She is not likely to know what she is capable of doing, nor to have the satisfaction of overcoming difficulties in the pursuit of either great or good ends." .

"She will never *have* to know, mother! She is rich." And I remember thinking, long ago, that riches have a certain miraculous power of buying off all the disagreeable things of life.

"The more is it to be regretted," answered my mother. "Nobody can ever go smoothly through this life. Trials and labour, at some time, they will certainly have. Happy for every girl, if she learns the great art of grappling with them while young. Then she will know how to make the best of those greater trials, which sooner or later come upon us all."

I could not feel what my mother said, at least so far as Cornelia was concerned. At any rate, I did not believe she would ever be obliged to lift a heavy tea-kettle over a blazing fire, with the hook swinging any way but the right one. Nor did I see any future good it could possibly do. I did not then know that even filling the tea-kettle helped to strengthen and educate the muscles of the body, to say nothing of acquiring a readiness and ease in those common and important household duties which young women nowadays are apt to esteem quite unworthy of them.

The older I grew, the more I thought of a suitable preparation for my future vocation. I became anxious to be thoroughly fitted for it, more thoroughly than the village school was capable of fitting me. Many a night witnessed me awake, planning and cogitating over what I should like to do; which was no less a plan than to go out of town to school. My heart was set upon going to D——, where, at that time, was a school of deservedly high reputation. The idea was a very bold one, and certainly would have appeared a very foolish one, had I revealed it. And so it seemed even to me in the daytime; but at night, while revolving in my mind all the advantages of such a movement, the thing sometimes looked near and practicable.

"How could I go?"

How? Yes, that was the question, and an extremely important preliminary to settle. At night, snug in bed, when everything seems easily done, I wondered if I could not earn enough in sewing, making shirts, or working muslin? It seemed as if, by a little extra industry, I might, not considering for a moment, perhaps, that it would take the making of all the shirts in the village, for a year or two to come, to pay my expenses. Then could I not sell milk enough? But almost everybody kept a cow, and the ready money arising from what little we did sell was never long on hand.

My desire to go to D—— was greatly increased, when Cornelia Gordon met me one day, begging me "to guess where she was going." She was "going away to spend the summer, and I must guess where!" Before giving fair play to my skill in that respect, she said it was "To D——. She was going to a boarding school!

Her mother said she learned nothing at home—
such miserable schools—and she was going to
try her away!"

"Yes, my mother says I shall go, and I mean
to try and get all the girls I can to go with me!
We will have such grand times! Sarah Day
says she thinks her father will let her go, and
the Mays and the Handys are going. Now,
Jane, you must go too! Can't you? We shall
want you to help us! I mean I shall," and her
pretty face was all glowing with excitement.

"Oh, I am having ever so many things made!
and I was going now up to your house, to see if
your mother can sew for us?"

She talked too fast for me to do anything but
exclaim, "Oh!" (and it did indeed appear so
to me,) "Oh! how delightful! Oh! fortunate
Cornelia!"

She came with me to our house, and found
my mother ready and thankful for the employ-
ment. She exclaimed, (after telling all the fine
things she was to have for the occasion,) "And
now, Mrs. Hudson, do let Jane go too, do! She
is such a good scholar, and my mother says we
have miserable schools here; and we shall have
such delightful times at the boarding school!
Do let Jane go with us!" And she pressed
coaxingly up to my mother's side.

My heart beat hurriedly! The thing was
proposed! plainly spoken out! I went to the
window to hide my face. It seemed as if the
first step was actually taken, and that, after all,
something would "turn up" in my favour. I
fancied the decision was near; it was near, and

I heard it plainly enough, as my mother gravely, perhaps sadly—a very little sadly—said, "Jane cannot afford to go, Cornelia. It costs a great deal of money to go out of town to school."

I am sure I could not have expected anything else, and yet it was a rough uprooting of all my night-waking wishes. Ah, it was not my first demolished air-castle, neither was it the last.

"But it will be so delightful!" persisted Cornelia. "Besides, if Jane is going to teach——"

"Delightful things are not always attainable, or desirable, my dear," said my mother. "If Jane will make a vigorous use of the means that are within her reach, the future will take care of itself."

I felt various emotions of disappointment—desire and envy, perhaps; and as I followed Cornelia to the door, my eyes resting upon her pretty new shawl, it seemed to me, that, if I were only Cornelia, I would certainly go out of town to school!

"Oh, mother," I said, whiningly, "if I only could go! Just think what the girls learn there! I shall never be fit for a teacher here! I wish, I do wish I could go!"

"No, Jane, you never will be fit for a teacher of others, if you suffer yourself to indulge in unavailing wishes, my child! Make the best use of the present, and the future will take care of itself! Be up and doing with what you have. See what improvement you can make this summer!"

"I will try, mother, that I will:" for her

good sense and cheerful tones always encouraged me. "Up and be doing! Up and be doing! shall be my motto."

It was my fourteenth spring, and every year increased my relish for study. The superior advantages which the other girls were about to enjoy stimulated me to new ardour, and I resolved, small as mine were, to improve them to the utmost. The village had usually sustained a small private school during the summer months, a few grades in advance of the public schools. Some of its last teachers failing to give satisfaction, wealthy parents looked elsewhere for their daughters' improvement. In consequence, five of the girls this season were destined for D——, making an important gap in our school circle. But I longed for it to begin! I longed to commence study.

The preparation and approaching departure of the five made quite a commotion in the village, and especially among all the girls. Those of us who were left could only look on and wonder, and wish, and admire. Amid it all, very little appeared to be saying or doing about our school.

"I must learn a great deal this summer, mother, for I must begin to teach soon!" As I looked into her face and beheld the furrows deepening under her incessant labours, I longed to be earning something to lessen them.

The next day, on returning home from an errand and meeting a companion, I eagerly inquired when school was going to begin.

"Why, there is to be no school this summer —no private one. They cannot get a teacher, and our old one will not come back without more scholars."

Such was Mary's unpleasant news. I ran home to communicate it to my mother.

" I am sorry," she answered; " but, as it is one of those things which we cannot control, we must not suffer ourselves to give way to unnecessary regrets. We will think what is best to be done; whether to return to the public school, or to continue your studies at home." She certainly looked very sorry.

Two days after, on a bright, pleasant April morning, the five girls rode by, in a stage-coach loaded with baggage, smiling and bowing, and shouting good-byes to everybody as they passed.

" Going to school is more necessary to me than to any of them, and yet here am I with no school at all!" and I dropped a tear on the faded calico sleeve, that was rolled up while I was washing the dishes.

" But I will study for all that, school or no school!" I exclaimed, resolutely. " Money buys schools, but it does not always buy a good education. Something more for that! It is the will and power to improve, mother says."

James was taken ill, and for some time my mother found no leisure to plan about studies. Meanwhile, every spare moment was given to my books; but I felt I was not making progress. It was at a time, too, when every hour was precious, and I felt a great thirst for knowledge.

" I must be up and doing!" I said, inwardly, a hundred times, whenever the lagging rate of my studies came into comparison with my desires; yet striving, all the while, to go about every household duty with quiet industry.

My aim was to be a teacher, and to be a good teacher; and that aim it became my fixed purpose, under the blessing of God, to reach. To further this, then, what was I to do, but patiently wait for an opening? No, not until my utmost efforts were made, then I could wait, and wait patiently. " Where there is a will, there is a way," mother says, and my energies were up and on the alert.

I began to look about once more for something I could do in order to earn the means of attending some good school—the Derry school, perhaps.

One day some one happened to say that the Green Lane school district was without a teacher. I knew the school was a small one, and composed principally of little children, at least in the summer season. The school-house was not more than a mile and a half from my home, presenting all the advantages of boarding at home, and helping mother in more ways than one; besides the pleasure of taking one of the pleasantest walks in the village. These were indeed advantages, and they rapidly passed through my mind.

" I will propose myself," was the instant conclusion. " What an opening!" There is no other district I could take; they are all so large! Really, it seems as if Providence had designed it for me. Oh, to be earning something!" And all that day a new alacrity was in every motion.

D

Assured of my mother's sanction, I concluded not to tell her of my good fortune, for it really seemed so just the thing, that I felt confident of success. And then, "such a capital opportunity of beginning to teach!" Yet I thought I would not tell her until I was sure—the engagement being actually made. But how was I to propose myself? Shall I call upon one of the committee, or send a note? I thought the latter less embarrassing, and never was note penned with greater care. Every *t* was crossed, every *i* dotted, and every stop made, with an exactness worthy of the occasion. The committee should at least see that the new candidate could write correctly. It was to be sent early in the evening and left at the door of the school committeeman, my courage not having risen high enough to run the smallest chance of meeting so important a personage in broad daylight.

How varied were my feelings on that solitary walk homeward! I had taken my first great step towards providing for myself, and assuming the new responsibility of helping our dear family. It seemed as if weighty matters were in progress. I was no longer a child. I felt that the abilities of womanhood were upon me. I longed to think and act in a larger sphere, and to be engaged in duties which would afford a wider scope to an earnest and awakened spirit. It did not seem to me I could fell another gusset or stitch another shirt bosom, at least without the prospect of going to school again.

When I went home, my mother was dressing Jemmy's foot, (Jemmy was a cripple,) and so busy was she, that I could only help her. Little

Mary was up. I took her in my lap and un-dressed her for bed, hearing her repeat the beautiful hymns with which our mother used to store our minds when we were yet very little. Mary appeared to me in a new aspect. I thought of her as my scholar!

On retiring to rest that night, the idea that I might soon go out into the world to act for my-self, oppressed me sorrowfully. For the first time it struck me that my mother's love and protection were not to be enjoyed everywhere, and I shrank from duties in which she had no part or lot. I seemed then to be feeling about, darkly enough, for that love, and help, and strength which the Father of our spirits can alone give us. I remember I arose, not to say my prayers again, but I kneeled down and prayed from a full, oppressed heart, that the God of my mother would be my God, that her Saviour would become my Saviour and my Friend. I felt the weakness and waywardness of my own nature, and could only say with the apostle, " I can do all things through CHRIST, which strengtheneth me."

The next day, as we sat together sewing, while Jemmy and Mary were by themselves, I opened to her the important matter which lay next to my heart—the desire I had for an edu-cation, and the steps I had taken in consequence of it. As I went on, I grew warmer.

" And now is not Green Lane just the open-ing I wanted? earning and learning to keep school too! Is it not, mother?"

She looked surprised, as she was apt to look, at any resolute advances of mine, my dreaming childhood giving little promise of vigorous effort. Oh, I owed it all to her training! She looked surprised, smiled, and acknowledged it did certainly seem very providential, if I could get the school, but bade me not to be too sanguine.

"Remember, Jane, we often need as much resolution to bear disappointments as we do to make efforts."

"But, mother, it seems just the niche for me to fill! You and Mary must come up and see me! And then to board at home too! Helping you, mother! Just think! It will be a beautiful walk for you to take, and the walk will do you good!"

Altogether it seemed the most probable thing in the world, despite my mother's warnings about a disappointment.

Ah, I did not then know all the difficulties of getting into office.

One—two—three—four days passed away, and no answer to my note. Was it ominous of good or evil? Every knock at the door fluttered me. A week gone, and no answer. I went out to do some shopping for my mother one day—the seventh from the note—when, behold, on turning a corner, the committee-man appeared on the opposite side! He looked hard at me. I felt like sinking to the earth, and then he crossed over:

"Is not this Miss Jane Hudson?" he asked, planting himself before me.

"Yes, sir."

"Well, you wrote me a note—I have been meaning to answer it. Yes, well—you wanted the Green Lane School?"

I am sure every light and shade of feeling must have been visible in my burning and anxious face.

" Yes, sir."

" Well, the fact is ! the fact is—" he smoothed down his red whiskers—" the fact is, Miss Jane ! I remember you at examination. You did well—" I took encouragement—" the fact is, I spoke to the rest of the committee about you, but—" he hemmed audibly—" but we think you are—too little !" and he looked down upon me with a perplexed and sorry air.

I received the announcement bravely. I neither wept nor whimpered, even by myself, but I felt the disappointment, to the innermost place of my heart.

" I know I am little, but I have a large spirit, and I feel that I can do !" So I ended the sub-jcet with my mother, drawing myself up an inch taller. " I should like to show Mr. Dow that little bodies can do something."

Thus ended my connexion with the Green Lane School.

Mr. Dow put in his niece, a very stout girl, who, if size were the chief requisite, promised extraordinary success.

———

And now what was to be done ? Was there anything else I could put my hand to ? any-thing, at least, which I was not too little to ac-complish ? My eye and ear were open. Again a path seemed in sight.

" Mother," said I, one Saturday evening,

after a long silence, " I like children, and now
I have a plan.   You know Mrs. Gordon talked
to-day about that lady who had come to pass
the summer in town, and she wanted very much
to find somebody to take care of her children.
Now, mother, am I not just the one, if she will
pay me for it?" still keeping my eyes upon the
same coals over which I had been ruminating,
for I did not know what reception my new plan
might meet with.

" Our Jane live out!" cried George, starting
up.   George had been passing a year at his
uncle's, and had come back with some notions
not quite corresponding to his situation.

" Our Jane live out!" he repeated,   " I hope,
mother, you will not let her do any such thing.
It seems to me Jane does not think much of
herself."

" I think enough of myself to wish to get a
good education, George," I answered; " and in
order to get that, I must work for it, in some
way or other."

" But living out!" he cried, scornfully.

" And what is the harm, George?" asked my
mother, placidly.

" Why, it's—it's—living out, mother!" reiterated George.

" Precisely so," said she, in the same tone;
" but where is the harm of Jane's taking every
honest means of getting a good education?"

" Every honourable means, mother; but I
do not think it would sound very well to have
it said, ' The Hudson girls have to live out.'
What would uncle's family say?"

" In the first place, we must look at our situation, just as it is, and judge of everything we do according to it."

Meanwhile, I was thankful mother had taken up the argument, for George would have driven me off, soon enough, by his bold assertions.

" We are poor, George. Industrious efforts to maintain ourselves are certainly more commendable than idleness : do you not think so ? "

George could not but admit it.

" You are all looking forward towards supporting yourselves—Jane, as well as her brothers. She has always thought of teaching as her business or profession, and we think she has talents and capacity, which, if properly cultivated, may fit her to be a good and useful teacher. But the best means of qualifying her for that calling are not within her reach, unless she is willing to make efforts to get them, or, in plain speech, to work for them. Now, how can any honest work, in the attainment of such an end, lower Jane in her own estimation, or in anybody's else ? Would it alter your opinion of Jane ? " she asked, looking at him with one of those looks of hers which meant so much.

George thought it would not ; but other people—what would they say ?

" Why, are they not capable of judging as sensibly as you, George ? "

George made no answer.

" But they will not," he muttered, at last ; " you know that, mother ! "

" If they judge foolishly, that is their look out, not Jane's. What she is to do is to go straightforward in the prosecution of her aims.

She has made up her mind what to do, and now she means to do it. Will Jane suffer in anybody's estimation, whose esteem is worth having, for acting thus?"

"No, mother, no!" cried James, eagerly.

"But, after all," continued she, "we must act for ourselves, and not be governed by other people's notions; and be sure, George, we shall never act independently, vigorously, and honestly, if we are looking more at what the world says, than we do at what God and our duty demand of us."

"But 'living out!'" persisted George, though in a less positive tone. "It seems to me there is something for Jane to do, besides 'living out!'"

"You know just how the matter stands," said I.

"'Living out' is only one branch of labour. I do not know of anything which degrades it, but the character of the labourer. Jane can preserve her integrity and self-respect as well in taking care of Mrs. Friendly's children, as in presiding at the Green Lane school; and she will have quite as good an opportunity of acquiring business habits, of learning the great art of self-control and self-sacrifice and patient effort, (so much needed in the world,) as she could have under any circumstances."

There was a pause. George sat twirling his two thumbs around each other; (his favourite mode of evincing perplexity;) James and I were looking at mother, who quietly sat in her chair, while the firelight danced in our faces, revealing lines of thought and solicitude.

"Then shall you let Jane go?" at length inquired George, looking up.

" Do you not think it is best for her, if thereby she is getting the means of advancing herself in her studies?" asked my mother, who always accustomed us to a free expression of our opinions, that she might be better enabled to set them right.

" I do not know but it would," answered he, somewhat reluctantly, evidently, if convinced at all, convinced very much against his will.

" But I want you to look the affair full in the face, George," she continued, " because it is an important matter to have right notions about. Instead of living week after week, month after month, and perhaps year after year, still finding herself no nearer the object of her wishes, anxious and dispirited, wishing and hoping, is it not far better for her to go resolutely to work—any honest work—in order to get the means of pushing forward her studies? With the means in her hand, you know, she can go on, and not till then. Everything before that must be at a stand-still. Both young men and young women are often brought to just such a pass, and, alas! they often shrink from it. They say, ' Why, I cannot do this,' and ' I cannot put my hand to that,' or ' What will people say?' and so are contented to sink into obscurity and uselessness, when a little independent exertion would place them in positions of trust and importance.

" What would you advise your sister to do, George?" asked my mother, not at all disposed to let him off. " Would you prefer to have her

sit and wait—at a period, too, when the improvement of her time is all-important—for
imaginary advantages, while real advantages,
however humble, can be secured?"

"I cannot say I should," replied he, "because Jane can be somebody anywhere, I suppose."

"She certainly can if she has good sense, and
resolution enough to meet her circumstances,
and not let her circumstances control her. If
she can rise superior to the foolish and often
false estimates of the world, and act with inde-
pendence and judgment, Jane can qualify herself for any situation.   It is not so much because
people have not the ability to do, that there are
so many weak and inefficient men and women in
the world, as it is the want of a proper indepen-
dence in acting up to what is really best for
them, as they themselves will acknowledge."

"If everybody would act as you talk, mother
—if everybody would only think so!"

"If only we ourselves will, George! Our
first and great duty is to act reasonably ourselves. The least we can do towards setting
the world right is to act rightly ourselves."

"Mother is right!" cried Jemmy, who had
been a most attentive listener. "Mother is
right!"

"Yes, mother is right," acknowledged George,
"and if everybody thought so too, there would
be some sense in it."   Poor George! "Everybody," in the shape of "what people will say,"
has ever been his bugbear, too often turning
him a great many points from the path of his
true interest.

Before the evening closed, it was unanimously decided that I should go and offer myself to Mrs. Friendly, to take care of her children. Then we each repeated a verse of Scripture, when our mother commended us to the God of mercy, praying that, whatever might be the scene of our earthly labours, we might spend our strength in the service of our Divine Master, and finally, through his rich grace, enter into his kingdom. With a " Good night," George and I left her.

As I put my arms around Mary, a sigh would come unbidden, at the. prospect of leaving her. I felt that I should love the little Friendly children for her sake.

———

When Monday morning came, I wished my mother would go and get the place for me. I shrank from an interview with the strange lady.

" I would willingly go for you, my child," said she, " but I want you early to learn to transact business for yourself; and now, while you are young, and while I am yet with you to give you counsel and sympathy, is your time to accustom yourself to business, to learn to go forward, and think and act and bargain for yourself. It must all come, and it is better to come early. Women are usually so deficient in these matters—in matters of fact, I mean."

So spake our mother. What a blessing have her counsels proved !

Dressed in my best, (a green cotton frock which the sun would fade, despite the most careful wearing,) I sallied forth on this new mission; as I went seeking to gird myself for the interview.

Reaching the house where she boarded, I inquired for Mrs. Friendly.

" She is out," was the answer, " but will be in soon."

I longed to ask who took care of the children. A noise attracted me as I ran down the steps, and looking up, a bright, curly-headed little girl was chirping at the window.

"I am sure, if that is one of the little Friendlys, I shall love her dearly. It will not be a hard task, if she is as good as she is pretty," and my heart warmed in prospect of the new occupation. After walking further and taking a turn round the corner, I again called.

Mrs. Friendly was still absent. Just as I was leaving the door, however, Mrs. Gordon came out.

" Ah, Jane, is this you, my dear? Did you wish to see Mrs. Friendly? She will be at home soon."

I will tell my errand to Mrs. Gordon, thought I. Perhaps this will open the way.

" I wanted to see," said I, faintly and timidly, " if Mrs. Friendly would engage me to come and take care of her children. I find I must do something this summer."

" You are a good child," said the lady, looking at me affectionately, " to wish to try and help your mother—a good child, Jane! I am always glad to see a spirit like this. But, my dear, I am sorry to tell you that a girl came from her sister's in ———, on Saturday night, and she came to live all summer with her."

" Never mind, Jane," she added, on beholding my disappointment, for I think a tear came
into my eye; " never mind! You will get
something else to do. There are more ways
than one to help your mother."

" But I wanted to earn something to go to
school with——"

" Did you, Jane? I wish from my heart
you were with Cornelia this moment. I am
sorry, my dear! It seems as if some way could
be devised for your going to D——! You
ought to go, I am sure. We will think of it."

Her kind and friendly manner—a manner
peculiar to Mrs. Gordon—softened, in some degree, the pang of the disappointment. " And I
am sure," thought I, " it is very evident that
she, so rich a lady as she is, does not think any
the less of me for trying to earn something, even
by ' living out.' Mother is right, that is plain."

Mrs. Gordon or the sweet June air quite re-
vived my spirits, and I returned home with a
lighter heart than could have been expected.
The sky, the trees, and the green wayside, reflected their images of beauty into my soul, and
I rejoiced in them, notwithstanding an early introduction into the struggles of life. But, fairly
in the little back kitchen, where my mother sat
by her huge basket of work, a keen sense of
disappointment came over me, and I sat down
and wept in good earnest.

" You must abide your time, my child,"
spake she, softly.

" How did you succeed?" " What success?"
" Are you going, Jane?" cried George, and
Jemmy, and Mary, as each successively came in

E

and wanted to hear all about it. I gave a minute account.

"Well, I am sorry!" exclaimed George, when the short recital was ended.

We were all quite amazed.

"Yes, I am sorry; for, the more I think of all mother said, the more true it seems; and then, Mrs. Gordon praised Jane for it!"

Ah, that was the secret! Mrs. Gordon was one of George's every-bodies.

"It is not to be!" said Jemmy.

"Oh, I am so glad!" and Mary clapped her hands and skipped about gladly.

"Now I think," said George, looking very wise, "that Mrs. Gordon will plan some way for your going to D——. Let us see. She said she wished you were with Cornelia. She said we will think of it. She asked if some way could not be thought of. Mrs. Gordon is rich, and she would not feel it to put her hand in her pocket and send Jane to D—— herself. Mother, was it not a hint for Jane to tell her what she wanted? It was a hint, mother! I think we shall hear more of it." And, as he looked around upon us all, his sparkling eyes and radiant face bespoke his own deep interest and sanguine hopes, as much as his words betrayed ignorance of the great world on whose threshold he as yet stood.

My mother looked at the ardent boy smilingly, and then gravely said, "Do not flatter Jane with hopes which will never be realized, George."

"Why, mother, it would be so easy for her just to put her thumb and finger into her purse, and then—out comes the money!" suiting the action to the word.

"I do really believe she will!" cried Jemmy; "Jane wants to go so."

"You will soon learn, my children, that people are not quite so disinterested as you think; neither must you build any hopes upon what you fancy people might do for you. Your only sure dependence, George and Jane, must be upon the blessing of God on your own honest hearts and industrious hands;" and she resumed her sewing.

"Well, mother, they might if they chose to do it. Rich people might do a great deal more good with their money than they do!" exclaimed George.

"That point you cannot undertake to decide until you know more facts in the case than you know now, George. It is easier to find fault with others than it is to live right ourselves."

I confess I leaned very much to George's suggestions, and could not help thinking that Mrs. Gordon's words meant something; yes, and that something would come out of them.

Several days passed in a state of pleasing suspense. A little hope glimmered, very little, yet enough to encourage an ardent temperament, with small experience of the world. I now know that kind words and friendly intimations are more intended to encourage our own efforts than to lead us to lean upon the arm of others.

Many days more passed, and nothing from Mrs. Gordon. Neither did she ever dream how much, for a season, were my first morning thoughts, and my last waking thoughts at night, turned towards her, in silent entreaty.

Now, indeed, I thought, I must patiently wait, realizing what my mother often said, " That it needs as much resolution to bear disappointments as it does to make efforts," and return to the

" Band, gusset, and seam,"

with many a longing, lingering look towards the schools from which I seemed to be shut out.

Eight months passed away, and I was verging towards fifteen. Meanwhile, the girls from Derry came home on vacation visits, pleased with their new school, and evidently much improved by it.

When Cornelia Gordon said she began to see through grammar, and a light upon fractions seemed to glimmer, Mary Sawyer declared that the new school possessed, in a remarkable degree, the power of giving sight to the blind; nor did we hear so much of the " good times" which Cornelia anticipated, at least so far only as they were connected with study and study hours.

Altogether, the girls came back to give a new impulse to our desires for knowledge, to make us feel more than ever our want of a good school, and deepen my anxiety to pursue my education under greater advantages.

Yet were not these eight months unimportant or unimproved. True, I did not go to school, but my mother had preserved some valuable books from the sale of her property, and these I read, conversing with my mother as I read, and reflecting much upon every subject to which they referred.

Under her watchful eye, I was constantly acquiring business habits, habits of order, regularity and promptness in every day's duties, acquired when young, if acquired at all. And then (it is a delightful remembrance to me now) we were all together, brothers and sisters, an unbroken band, happy in each other's love, and constant in our endeavours to aid and improve each other; the pressure of poverty, if it could be called poverty, binding us closer and closer together.

It was the last year we ever passed together.

As my fifteenth spring opened, I began to look around for something to do, resolving with patient endeavour to do with my might whatsoever my hand found to do. Towards school-keeping my eyes still anxiously turned.

One day in March, the farmer who usually brought wood for us from a neighbouring village made his appearance in the yard with a fine load of hemlock.

" There is Mr. Sykes !" cried Jemmy.

" We do not especially need that wood; besides, I owe him a little on the last," said my mother, rummaging for her pocket-book.

She went out to him. In a long discourse about the wood, the wind and weather coming in for a share (for Mr. Sykes was in no hurry to do business, besides feeling himself privileged to talk with my mother, from long acquaintance with her father), I heard him ask :

" Well, have you any good school-mistresses

down here? I want to get one for our district
—a real good one!"

"*I am that!*" I cried, starting up, as the
words came through the porch. "Who will
not call this an opening? Is it not, Jemmy?"
and I ran to the porch door to hear mother's
answer.

She encouraged him with the probability
that a school-mistress could be found for his
district, such as he desired.

Shall I run out and propose myself, or—or—
or—? darted through my mind. I decided
upon *or*, as the most dignified way of conduct-
ing the matter. In a word, I remembered that
Mr. Sykes was a brother to our good friend
Sykes, who perhaps would recommend me.
My mother decided favourably upon the wood.

As soon as she reappeared, "Mother!" I
exclaimed excitedly, "did you think of me?
Shall not I take that school? Is not that an
opening? And is it not providential that he
spoke to us upon the subject first? We can
be first on the carpet!"

"There is nothing like trying, Jane, though
I will not determine how far you answer the
description," said my mother, smiling.

"And I can apply to Sykes, mother, and he
can recommend me to his brother. It seems so
providential, too, that our friend is his brother,
because he is so kind to us. He will aid me,
I know!" Thus ran my thoughts.

"It certainly is a spoke in the wheel, is it
not, mother, farmer Sykes and Mr. Sykes
being brothers?" said Jemmy, looking up from

his work, with great interest. Though Jemmy could engage in no out-of-door sports and duties like other boys, in many ways he made himself useful within. He was then braiding a palm-leaf hat. Making palm-leaf hats for several years was a great business with him, affording at once a pleasant occupation and the means of adding his mite to the family funds.

"It certainly is a spoke," said my mother.

As usual, a full discussion of farmer Sykes's inquiry took place at the evening fireside, and the decision was unanimous that it was an opening which I had better try to fill.

"His brother will befriend you, Jane, I know; and I will go myself and ask him to recommend you!" said George.

"No — let Jane apply herself," said my mother. "It is important for her to get accustomed to business matters, you know."

And, not many days afterwards, I sallied out in quest of Mr. Sykes. He was a blacksmith, and morning, night, and noon saw him toiling at the anvil. There must he be sought, for I knew I should have more courage, and could speak more freely with him alone, than in the presence of his family; and seeing him was in every respect preferable to writing. Past disappointments in no degree damped the new expectations and new efforts upon which I was entering. Circumstances compelled me to action, and I was up and ready to act heartily.

Coming in sight of Mr. Sykes's little black shop, holding somewhat of a conspicuous position at the corner of a street and lane, my feet lagged and my heart beat quickly. To revive my courage and gain strength for the interview, I decided to cross over and pass by on the other side, reconnoitering the premises, to see if all things were favourable. Neither horse nor ox was waiting to be shod; neither cart, wagon, nor man occupied the coal-trodden stand before the door of the smithy. A secret hope lurked within, that something or somebody would appear to prevent or at least delay the meeting. But no, the way was never clearer. Nobody in sight or hearing but one of his little boys, playing hide-and-seek with a dog between two old cart-wheels, standing against the left side of the shop. "Now is the time," I cried quickly, and quickly turned about upon my errand, hastening up to the little fellow, and asking him to call his father to the door a moment. He scampered in—the dog after him.

"Courage," I said, trying to feel unconcerned; and, in order to do so, turning my attention upon the little brooks, muddy and babbling, being set in motion by the March thaw, that were running down the lane—"courage!"

It was but for a moment.

"Here is father!" cried the little boy at my elbow.

I looked suddenly around, and beheld "father," in his leather apron, shirt-sleeves rolled up, and his face lighted up by one of the kindest smiles in the world. It was just the face to ask a favour of, and I felt sure that I should be successful.

"Ho! ho!" cried he. "I didn't know I was

going to meet a lady. Not in good trim, but just as glad to see you for all that. How is your mother, Jane?"

Answering for her good health, I coughed and hemmed, and at last came out with my business, my courage rising, as I went on, at the pleased and interested expression upon his countenance.

"Yes, yes! that I will! I will give you a recommendation!" A slight and pleasant motion of the head. "Your examination! I remember hearing of it. It was you that wrote that piece about the town. Yes, yes! I will send word to my brother. But stop. I am going over in a day or two, and I will see to it all myself. It is a good place! They think a good deal of their school-mistresses! I will see to it myself, Miss Jane!" And I knew that he would.

"Is not Mr. Sykes a good man, mother?" inquired Mary, after recounting the afternoon's adventure for the second time, when we were all reassembled around the fire, after tea. "And little Sarah Sykes is just like him. All the girls at school love her dearly."

"I always liked him," said Jemmy. "It was really kind in him to say he would see to it all himself. And, mother, do you not know how he has taken me out to ride when I was ill?"

My mother nodded assent.

"Yes, and when he comes to the shop he never beats us down; wanting Mr. Emery to take less than he gave for it, as some people do! He bargains like a man!" exclaimed George, spiritedly.

George was now in Mr. Emery's shop. My mother had destined him for a trade, but that gentleman thought he discovered in my brother an aptitude for business, which greatly pleased him. He talked with our mother, and, making her a generous offer for his services, George soon took his place behind the counter.

George told several pleasant stories of Mr. Sykes's kindness and readiness to help, that he had heard at Mr. Emery's, the truth of which was corroborated by instances of a similar nature within our own family history. Indeed, never was there a kinder friend. The whole village felt his benevolent spirit. Mr. Sykes was decidedly the hero of the evening; and we retired, well satisfied that our plans were in safe keeping.

What was to be the result? I looked anxiously forward.

AN ERA.

THE sabbath evening was a delightful season in our little circle. There were no evening meetings, in those days, to take us from home. We never visited, and seldom received visits, except perhaps the occasional call of some good man, to inquire after the moral or religious welfare of my mother's little flock, and to proffer her his Christian sympathies. We usually reviewed the catechism, repeated hymns, rehearsed all we could remember of the sermons, and sang together. I cannot even now listen to Old Hundred, or Mear, or Wells, or Windham, or St. Ann's, or St. Martin's, without a homesick longing for those blessed times, those precious old times, when our voices all joined together, making the little back sitting-room echo with the melody of Jehovah's praise. There was my mother in her arm-chair at one corner; Jemmy opposite her, in his low chair; Mary on a seat by my mother's side, her little hands clasping one of mother's, while George and I were at the candle-stand, with our books, presiding over the order of the hour, whether singing or reciting, a small tallow candle of home-manufacture flaming or flickering over our pages. What a cheerful radiance and warmth did the fire-light then impart, flinging our shadows on the wall, while brightening our faces and warming our feet, and casting the little tallow candle quite in the background. The sabbath evening was never a dull or joyless evening to any one of us. While it was truly a day and evening of rest—rest from the needle, the kitchen, and the counter; rest from toil—it was also a day of activity, of progress, of improvement.

Every book and engagement was appropriate to the sacredness of the occasion; and yet, under our mother's judicious training, nothing was wearisome or spiritless, as sabbath-day exercises are so often, even to children of pious parents.

We were singing

"Thine earthly sabbaths, Lord, we love,"

a favourite hymn of mother's, when, lo! a knock at the door.

Mary smoothed down her apron, drawing her

seat closer to her mother; Jemmy drew himself up on his couch; I snuffed the candle; while George answered to the summons, soon ushering in Mr. Sykes.

How glad we all were to see him! I can now see the flush of pleasure mount into Jemmy's pale face, as Mr. Sykes folded his hard, bony hand around the thin, shadowy fingers of the sick child, and said: " Ah, here is my old friend James! Well, my boy, we must have another ride together, before the snow all goes!"

As for me, my hand trembled when he took it, for I felt that my destinies were in his hands, rough and hard as they were, and that his present call was in some way blended with them. I remember I slipped out of the room into the porch, to suppress the agitation which I began to feel at the possible result of his application or " recommendation."

Back in my chair again, he turned round and looked meaningly at me.

" Now it is coming," thought I; "let me receive it courageously, good or bad. I am a year older and taller."

" Well, Jane," (he began so good humouredly, that I was sure he had good news. Then turning to mother,) " So, Mrs. Hudson, your daughter Jane is going to be a school-mistress, is she?"

" If you can see fit to recommend her to a situation, Mr. Sykes," said my mother, smiling.

" I can, Mrs. Hudson, and I have. I told my brother about her," and—and—and—the good man's story was probably more interesting to the little group which then listened than it

can be to my readers now. Suffice it to say,
that no other teacher had been thought of;
that my offer was before them, with Mr. Sykes
to support me, one whose wise judgment on
general matters entitled his judgment upon
school-mistresses to no inconsiderable degree
of respect among his peers.

For some days I felt that I was almost as
sure as if I had been in the school-house with
the children around me.

Who would come for me? How should I
go? How much would they give me? were
interesting questions, often agitating our little
kitchen. Every day I took my seat at the
window, in the direction whence farmer Sykes
and his wood usually made their first appearance, to watch his arrival, or the arrival of some
messenger to apprize me of my success.

Seven days did I watch in vain. Neither
horse nor wagon stopped at our gate, and my
heart began to sink at the possibility of another
disappointment. On the eighth day I took my
seat by my mother at the little stand, resolving
to abide the event with firmness and patience.
And it was sew! sew! sew! while Jemmy sat
beside us, sometimes writing on his slate, sometimes reading us a story.

A knock at the porch door.

" Let me go!" said Jemmy. " Oh, mother,
I wish I could run like other boys! I am so, *so*
tired!" He took his cane and hobbled to the
door.

" Is your mother in, or your sister? Your
eldest sister I think I want." It was Farmer
Sykes's voice.

"Mother! mother!" I whispered, hastily striving to keep down the rising agitation. Jemmy ushered him in.

In about half an hour my fate was decided! I was school-mistress elect of district No. 1, in the little village of ——. Oh, it was the proudest and happiest hour of my life! Success had at last crowned my efforts.

The good news was duly proclaimed to George and Mary, as soon as they reached home; and, in spite of the work we had to do, I could not resist stealing twenty minutes, after washing the dishes, to look into my grammar, and also to see just how far I had gone in arithmetic.

In the third week in May, two important departures took place. Cornelia Gordon and her companions returned to D——, and I, myself, went to ——.

A few days before Cornelia went, I took some work home which we had done for Mrs. Gordon.

"Oh, come up stairs!" cried Cornelia. "Sarah May is here. I am beginning to pack up!"

And well she might begin in season, for she had more dresses about the room than I ever had in my life.

"Here is my new dress, Jane; is it not a beauty?" she cried. "And my yellow crape! I teased mother for this yellow crape! None of the girls will have any thing prettier than that; and you know you brought home my two new white dresses!" And she ran on, displaying her ample wardrobe with the greatest good nature.

"Oh, Jane, I wish you were going to D——!

It is too bad that your mother will not let you."

" My mother cannot afford it," I answered, gravely.

" Cannot afford it! Cannot afford it! So my father often says. But he can afford it. We always get out of him—mother and I—just what we want; so I do not believe in ' cannot afford it.'"

Cornelia spoke truly. She probably had never a wish denied.

" Why, Jane is going to keep school!" said Sarah.

" Keep school!" exclaimed Cornelia. " Bless me! Such a little thing as she is! Why, Jane, you ought to *go* to school! What upon earth does your mother let you keep school for? Why, you will die if you keep school. You ought to go to school, I say! Jane keep school!" and Cornelia burst into a loud laugh.

I was at a stand. The yellow crape dress fell from my hand. I did not know whether to cry or laugh with her. Was she making fun of me? Did she think I did not know enough, or that the scholars would not obey me? I felt angry and mortified. That a position so long sought, so ardently desired, should be treated in this way was extremely painful to me.

" I must be unfit for it. They think I shall never get through with it. They think I do not know enough. It will be a failure!" All these thoughts passed rapidly through my mind, filling my eyes with tears, and sinking my spirits.

" Jane a school-mistress! Why, they will not mind you, Jane," cried Cornelia. " You must get a stick bigger than you are." Cornelia was privileged to say and act just as she pleased among her companions. Had any one else dared to treat my new prospects in a way like this, I should have hardly borne it.

"Well, I think your mother ought to send you to school," declared she, her mirth having in some good degree subsided. "That is what I think!"

"My mother has no money to pay my bills at school. We are poor. She would be very glad to have me go, as glad as I should be to go, but I keep school now, to get money. I must get my own living, and I want to do it by teaching. I must begin in a small way, and then work my way up, if I can." This was a great deal for me to say, in my excited state of mind.

"How much do they pay you, Jane?" asked Sarah.

"Ten shillings a week, and my board found; In twelve weeks, you see, I shall earn six pounds,"—a sum which I expected would amaze my companions, as it did Jemmy and me, as we reckoned it up and repeated it over.

"Only a little more than what my new crape and trimmings came to," cried Cornelia; "and you have to work twelve long weeks for it!"

I was discouraged. "How differently the same things look to different people!" I thought. The sum which seemed so large, and the opportunity which seemed so providential for earning it, in our little back kitchen, with an invalid brother on one side and a mother hard at work on the other, dwindled rapidly down to nothing in-

Mrs. Gordon's best chamber, strewed all over with beautiful things, and beside a yellow crape which cost almost as much. I soon left the room, in no way improved by the short visit up stairs.

"Oh, I wish I were as well off," said I, as I passed through the long entry on my way out. "I—poor I! I have to work every inch of my way!"

On returning home, I felt little inclined either for speaking or working. Everything looked hard and up-hill. I wondered why the Gordons were so rich and we so poor, and felt dis-·posed to murmur and be unthankful.

"Mother," I said, towards the close of a speechless hour—"mother, Cornelia Gordon has such beautiful things! Her new yellow crape cost almost as much as my whole summer's work will come to!"

"But her money does not buy things half as valuable as yours will. You have a secret that she has never learned. The possession of such a secret is even greater than the possession of money."

I looked inquiringly up, at this unexpected turn of the matter. "What is so great as money, mother?"

"KNOWING HOW TO USE IT," she answered, slowly and quietly.

"I am sure there is nothing difficult in that, mother!"

"On the contrary, it is one of the most difficult things in the world, Jane! There is nothing like scanty means to teach one to distinguish between what is really necessary and important for

us, and what is not. This knowledge, wisely
improved, will put you in a way of spending
your money to the best advantage; at the same
time, if your money is dearly earned, you will
be so much the less likely to part with it, unless.
for something really worth it."

I pondered for some time.

" Oh, mother, I think they ought to give me
more than ten shillings a week—only six pounds
for a whole summer! How easy Cornelia can
get six pounds! She only has to ask for it!"
It was peevishly spoken.

" While you must work for it, Jane," added
my mother.

" Work! work! Nothing but work for me.
None of the other girls know what work is!"
And I was as discontented as I could well be.

" And what is the evil or the harm of working, Jane?" she asked, in one of her quietest
tones. I made no answer.

" The fact is, Jane," she continued, earnestly,
" everybody has something to do. God did
not place us here to be idle. He has given to
each one—to you and to me, to George and to
James—a work to accomplish, a work of some
kind. Yours is fairly before you. You can see
it and measure it, and in some degree can look
forward to results. Your school this summer,
if you have the courage and ability to sustain it,
will enable you to get a better education; a
better education will entitle you to a wider sphere
of action, and on—and on—we know not the
end. Instead of measuring yourself by others,
who have apparently less before them, and then
grumbling, and shrinking, and holding back,.

and growing dissatisfied and disheartened, GO
FORWARD and GRAPPLE with your work courageously, heartily, with patience and industry.
You can never get away from your present situation, but by persevering efforts. Look, then,
straight at it. Not a ' What this one has, or that
one,' but keep your eye fixed on present duty,
and attend to it. Can you not do that, Jane ?
Can you not be up and doing with a cheerful
energy ? Work is no drudgery to her who has
resolution ; it is only a bugbear to the idle and
irresolute."

I knew she was sustained by a trustful reli-
ance on a covenant God, and that she was willing to receive the allotments of his providence
as the very best that could happen to her. It
was no stoical effort to brave difficulties, but a
simple confidence that all things shall work together for good to those who are the children of
God in Christ Jesus. It was with such a faith
that she strove to have us armed.

" It certainly does not seem a bugbear in
your hands, mother!"

One of her pauses ensued, when she meant I
should reflect.

" What is Cornelia's work?" I asked, finding it not so easy to forget Cornelia's case.

" I do not know. Sooner or later our work
all comes to us," she answered.

My mother's words of wisdom were not always
easily received; but they did fasten themselves
upon us, and in process of time, like leaven,
worked themselves into our hearts, and produced fruit in our lives. The great secret was,
that she lived up to the rules she prescribed for

us. She never suffered herself to be appalled or disheartened by the most adverse or discouraging circumstances; but wisely, patiently, and cheerfully wrought out for herself and little ones a path, a good path—a path which, if it had thorns, had roses also, and led to right results.

On a bright, cool Saturday afternoon, a boy drove his wagon into our yard, to take me away to the scene of my future labours. A small box contained my simple wardrobe; a new cotton dress for Sundays, my faded green for every day, with a few other necessary articles, completed the list, except a black silk which I had on, and which was an old one of my mother's, newly dyed. We were all in the sitting-room, where, as a parting courtesy, a small fire had been kindled before dinner. George caught up the box and ran to stow it away in the hinder part of the wagon. I drew my shawl closely around me, and looked about to see if anything were missing or unthought of. Ah, it was to hide the struggle, as I began vividly to realize that I was indeed going away from home! Mary hugged my bundle of books in her arms. "I will carry these! I will carry them, and give them to you after you are in."

Jemmy went to the window. I beheld him quickly rubbing the back of his hand across his eyes; and my mother, always thoughtful and at work, my mother was fixing an old umbrella, which she was sure I should need, and which they must contrive to spare me. Placing it in my hand, "There, Jane," she said, cheerfully, for a sob from Jemmy had just brought tears into

Mary's eyes; "now all is ready. You will have a fine ride! I wish we were all going to have one. And then, in a month, you will spend Sunday with us. Mr. Sykes promises that! Only a month! Behave like a woman, Jane. Do not be afraid of small trials. God bless you, my daughter!" There was a slight agitation betrayed in her voice, and then she kissed me. Then there were kisses to Jemmy and Mary, mingled with tears.

"Come, Jenny," cried George, "I will help you into your carriage. Ah, you may be good, but you will never be great," he declared, laughingly. "She will never be great if she is only a school-mistress, will she, mother?"

"You come to my school, and I will show you what I can do, Master George," said I, hastening away.

I tripped as I got into the wagon. Mother ran out to ascertain if all was right. Mary got upon the wheel to hand me the bundle of books. George again jumped up behind, to see if the box was safe. All was snugly packed. The driver took his place by my side. I looked around for Jemmy. There he still stood at the window, neither speaking nor moving, but looking sadly pale.

Good-by! good-by! good-by!

I kissed my hand again and again to the dear ones, never dearer, as we turned away from the door. Just going out of sight, I turned round for one more glance at the old house. Mary was stretching her neck out at the gate, looking after me. Still at the window was Jemmy. I waved my handkerchief. Dear, dear sick brother, I know he will miss me!

I was now out upon the wide world, alone. Never before from home or away from my mother's counsel, I was now to push my way among strangers, teaching, admonishing, counselling, correcting, and chastening dozens of untutored minds, and ruling, not only over others, but over the untried powers of my own spirit.

I did not then know the magnitude of the work before me. Happy for us, that our work, which seen in the bulk must overpower us, is meted out to us in seconds and minutes, and hours and days, each bearing its own burden.

A few days completed my fifteenth year.

NEW SCENES—SCHOOL-KEEPING.

It did not take me long to see that the schoolmistress was an object of no little importance in the district. The best bed-room in Mr. Green's house was awarded to her, with nicely sanded floor and braided mat at the bedside; two ostrich feathers over the glass, and a large bunch of spruce in the chimney.

She was honoured with an extra muffin at breakfast and cake at noon, at the expense of having eight laughing eyes turned towards her plate, from four little Greens at the foot of the table. And then, how pleasant was the walk down the hill, by the road-side, under the shade of the apple-trees and three young oaks. The school-house, black and rickety, stood a quarter of a mile off, in the sunniest corner, where two

roads met, with eight staring windows, into
which the sun generously poured his beams, un-
interrupted by tree or shrub, or curtain or blind.
On one side was a cranberry meadow; on the
other, not a long way off, were groves of pines,
among which the summer winds made grave
and gentle melody. Two or three houses were
in sight, and many columns of smoke issued
from behind hill and hollow, betraying the scat-
tered homes of my little flock. But it was still,
very still. An occasional cart or wagon was
heard, and the mail-stage passed once a day.
These, with the lowing of a cow and the barking
of a dog, were the chief interruptions of the
deep quiet of the district; except, indeed, when
school was let out. Then a brief shouting, and
one by one, boy and girl, singly or in groups,
disappeared (as if by magic) behind the scenes,
down a lane one way, or through the woods another.

The school-room was my world, and the world
in miniature, with all its restlessness, and pas-
sions, and curious devices; and the world, too,
as a place of trial and discipline. With elbow
upon the worn pine desk, how often did I press
my throbbing forehead into my hand, to recover
from the anger stirred up by impudence and dis-
obedience; the impatience provoked by idleness
and dulness, and the strength wasted by toil. I
knew I must be calm, and there would I sit, and
not speak until the tempest of inward feeling
had subsided.

Among the thirty children (mostly girls)
which composed the school, I was startled by

the size of one of the boys, a large boy, larger than myself, with an off-hand, daring expression, and a swagger which seemed to say, "I am myself, and who are you?"

Mr. Sykes had assured us that all the large boys forsook schooling for farming during the summer, leaving the way open for all the little ones. I certainly did not like the appearance of Timothy, so unlike his great namesake, good Timothy of old. In speaking of the matter to Mr. Green, he said: "Well, you would be as well off without him, but his father wants Tim to get learning. He will never make a farmer. You must get on with him as easily as you can. They are well off."

This intelligence was not fitted to quiet my fears or anxiety, or recommend Tim to further favour. However, I meant to do my best, and if possible secure Tim on my side by kindness, and especially to keep him employed by pushing him on in his studies.

For awhile things went smoothly on. Tim seemed to be thrown upon his good behaviour, and the children appeared disposed to join hands with their new mistress in the march of improvement. The new mistress entered into all her duties with cheerfulness and courage, deeply interested, and greatly gratified by every symptom of improvement. So things went on for nearly three weeks, when signs of disorder began to be manifest. There was more shuffling among the boys, and occasional twittering. Paper balls began to be thrown, and a great iron andiron was found posted in the mistress's seat, as grave and prim as could be; besides sundry other movements that indicated an insubordinate spirit. On inquiry, it was found that "nobody did it," and "nobody knew anything about it."

As for Tim, I kept my eye upon him, and, though I thought I watched him closely, I could never detect him in mischief. He seemed hard and soberly at work over his books. Indeed, I began to feel that he was conquered, and that I had really found the secret of subduing and influencing one of the worst boys in the district.

"Well, how does Tim behave?" asked Mr. Green, one day.

"As good a boy as need be!" I answered, a little proudly perhaps.

"Does he not trouble you? For you are the first master or mistress that we ever had yet, that he did not come nigh plaguing their lives out."

I began to think more than ever that I was entitled to be considered a superior teacher.

Soon there were more disorders in school, but nobody was at the bottom of them. The reins of authority were drawn tighter, yet I did not seem to reach the mischief. I was vigilant and resolved, often wearied, but often refreshed.

It was on Friday of a hard week, and I was going slowly to school, girding myself up as I went along, when, from a little hillock by the wayside, I felt my dress suddenly pulled. I had not noticed that one of my little girls sat there.

"Stop a moment, ma'am," she whispered,

thrusting a piece of mince pie into my hand,
wrapped up in brown paper; love tokens of
this kind being not unusual.

I thanked little Sally.

"Stop, ma'am," she whispered, dodging down
again. "Tim has laid a trap at the school-room
door for you to fall over, when you go in. I
thought I would tell you about it."

"Who," asked I, eagerly—"who did you
say had done it, Sally?"

"It is Tim, that boy that put the irons in
your chair, and does all such sorts of things. It
is Tim who does them."

I thanked Sally cordially, and kissed her
cheek. She was an affectionate little creature,
and prized nothing so much as a kind notice
from the school-mistress. I felt that she had
now repaid fourfold all the pleasant words I
had ever given her.

"Please, ma'am," said she, as I was hastening on, "don't tell it's I who told you, because all the girls are afraid of Tim." I assured her of secrecy.

Arrived at the school-house, I carefully opened
the door. I discovered the cords placed across
in a way to trip up any unwary steps. The
children were all assembled and in their seats,
evidently expecting to enjoy the sight of the
school-mistress tumbling in. As it was, it was
with some embarrassment to my dress that I
stepped over. There was a sensation in the
room, but I cannot describe it. Tim was
perched up in the highest seat, ciphering.

I felt grieved at such poor, thankless returns
for all my efforts for him, and saw that I must

now do something to nip in the bud future disorders.

When the recess came, I called Timothy, and
directed him to unfasten and remove the cords
at the door, before any one could go out. He
looked startled, but sat still. In recalling and
recording this circumstance, the wisdom of my
first proceedings might be questioned, but let
every one remember it was the wisdom of but
fifteen years.

" Remove those cords, Timothy," I again
repeated.

Timothy did not budge. I felt that I did
not deserve this at Timothy's hands.

My heart throbbed. Then I told the scholars
what a source of regret it was to me that there
were those among them disposed to bring disorders into the school; that every such attack
was in reality an attack upon their real interests,
and an attempt to betray them into weak and
foolish conduct; that I wanted their cheerful
and hearty cooperation. I talked some time,
until I could perceive on every face, and in
every eye, public opinion in my favour. " And
now it is but fair," I added, " that he who laid
the snare should step firmly forth and undo it."
The children looked anxious.

" I want to see the boy who does this, under
the mistaken idea that it is a good joke, come
forward and honourably acknowledge his fault
by removing the cords."

Timothy looked sheepish and guilty, but
moved not. Increasing anxiety was apparent
among the scholars.

" It is now time for the recess. If he does not

obey, we cannot allow him to be a scholar here until he comes and makes a public acknowledgment of his faults and asks our forgiveness."

I gave the recess. Timothy rushed across the seats, and, jumping over the cords, was out in a minute.

"I ask forgiveness!" he shouted. "I! not I! But I shall come back to school! Father will see to that! No master or mistress ever put me down yet!"

The many children who remained behind looked anxiously towards the desk, to see if I had heard. Yes, I had heard. Timothy remained all day; but I took no notice of him, and heard none of his lessons.

In relating the circumstance to Mr. Green when I went home, "Ah," he said, "I am sorry. It is of no use! He will get the upper hand of you! There is no breaking Tim, for his father backs him."

"But will not the committee help me to establish my authority, and turn a disorderly boy out of school if he does not obey?"

"The fact is, his father pays a good part of the tax, and we do not want to offend him. I am afraid you will not do much with him."

"I will see the committee this very evening. My mother says, 'Never give up.'"

And as soon as supper was over away I trudged to two neighbouring farms, to learn what was to be expected from the two committeemen.

The answer was substantially the same as Mr. Green's.

"We should be glad to help you, very glad to

help you," they said; " but we do not want to get
into a quarrel with Tim's father. His father is
a hard man."

" I should have been glad for you not to have
been quite so severe, though Tim deserves it
five times over—a flogging once a day! As it
is, though, I suppose you must ease off a little."

" But what an injury will such an example
be to the school! How it will let down lawful
authority and give room to a thousand other
disorders!" I persisted. It was of no use.
The committee knew it all, but they were afraid
to act.

It was quite dark by the time I returned,
and I went my way painfully solicitous for the
event, and longing for my mother's counsel.

" What course shall I adopt?" I awoke a
dozen times in the night with this question.

The next day Tim appeared in school with a
bold, defying air. I took no notice of him.
Contrary to my expectations and fears, most of
the boys arrayed themselves against him, and
manfully resisted all his attempts to draw them
into play during school-hours.

The next, and next, and next day came and
passed, and Tim could not relish the utter
neglect with which he was treated. The next
day he came in half an hour after school began,
and brought me a message from his father, to
the effect that, if his lessons were not recited, he
would come and see to it himself—the dreadful
father, of whom the committeemen stood in
such fear!

" Shall I give up? Shall I? So young
and so small, what can I do alone?" And I

did not know whether the class before me were spelling wright or wrong, or at all, until some one said :

"Ma'am, Peter did not put any *a* in soak."

This recalled me to myself; and "Never give up!" was the second sober decision, after the class was through. My mother says, "Never give up in an important purpose! Giving up now would be such a hindrance to my government! No, I will not give up!" and I am sure I must have been an inch or two taller after the resolution.

But what was to be done? Whatever I did must be done upon my own responsibility, unaided and unbacked. It was Saturday afternoon, and I determined to visit Tim's father myself, and "brave the lion in his den," and lay the case before him, demanding his cooperation and authority.

"Never do it!" cried Mrs. Green. "He is a singular man! I will tell Mr. Green."

"I wish you success," said Mr. Green, "but I cannot promise it to you."

"I cannot advise you to go," he came back and said. "Saturday afternoon he is as cross as a crab! and it is a dull place where he lives."

But the matter must be concluded, and I was not to be dissuaded. It must be confessed I turned down the dark lane, with woods on either side, leading to Mr. Pott's house, with no enviable feelings. Once I stopped, and hesitatingly sat down upon a rock.

"Oh, home, home!" I sighed. "Why not let the matter go? I shall be here but seven weeks longer! Why trouble myself with it?

Oh, home! mother! I wish I could live at home!" And tears began to come, as I sat there alone, and in the woods, on my way I hardly knew whither.

"Fight through your difficulties courage-ously!" "Grapple with your duties!" "Never give up!" I seemed to hear my mother say through the woods. "Try! Try! Try, Jane! Do your best!" and the very pines seemed to echo "Try!" And then, as I sat and thought, I felt I had rather return to my mother and tell my story, conscious of a well-fought battle, even if beaten, than seem weak and infirm of purpose.

Then I went further into the woods and kneeled down upon the dead leaves of the forest, and prayed! Yes, I did really and truly pray. I felt that I needed strength, and my mother's God and Saviour could grant it. I needed protection, and He could vouchsafe it. I needed wisdom, and He could bestow it. I then felt (perhaps for the first time) how blind, and poor, and wretched, and naked, and in need of all things, is the human heart alone, in itself. I longed for a union, by faith, with that Almighty Friend and Redeemer, who will always afford his children strength equal to their day.

I know not how long I remained there, but long enough to go (when I did go) with a calm and cheerful courage. Down wound the lane a mile and a half through the woods, until it came to an opening, with a house, and sheds, and barns, and all the appendages of a large farm. No one was in sight. I approached the door and knocked. An old woman opened it. On inquiring for Mr. Potts, she said he was "out in the field, over there," pointing with her finger.

"When will he come in?"

"When he gets his work done!" was the crabbed reply, auguring nothing very pleasant.

She did not ask me in nor offer me a seat. What was to be done? Not daunted by so inauspicious a beginning, I determined to have the matter settled, and to seek an interview with Mr. Potts in his field. She pointed out to me the probable direction. Over the fence I jumped, and across the fields I sped till on a mound I discovered three men, one sitting apart under a tree, with a mug in his hand. The three espied me at the same moment, and stared with wonder.

"Courage," I repeated a hundred times, making my way to the man under the tree. He drank and stared as I approached. Anybody who had ever seen Tim would have recognised his father. I actually shrank from his bold, sharp, mahogany face.

"Good afternoon, Mr. Potts," I said, earnestly; "I suppose you know me—Miss Hudson, the school-mistress."

"He did not know how upon earth he should know the school-mistress," he said; "he had only heard tell of her; but, if she was the one, he had a thing or two to say to her!"

How long we talked, and all that we said, I cannot now remember; but the sun was near setting before we turned and walked towards the house. He civilly took down the bars to let me into the yard, and invited me in. I thought I must go.

"Well, call some other time, then. I will go down the lane with you a little way. Miss Hudson"—he stopped, and so I stopped— "Miss Hudson, you are the first master or school-mistress that ever came and talked reasonably to me about that boy," and tears started into the father's eyes. "He leans to you—he does, Miss Hudson! You are good to him, and he *shall* mind you. I will fetch him myself, and he shall do just what you want him to do. It is in him to do right. He likes you, but somehow he gets into trouble. He shall do! he shall! he shall! Miss Hudson, he shall mind you. Tim shall! For you are the best and most reasonable instructor Tim ever had. All the rest rear up so and fluster, setting the whole district astir about my boy."

As he stood before me in that lonely lane, with the tall, dark pines on either side, his old palm-leaf hat thrown back, the long shaggy hair that escaped on every side over his ears and shoulders, his stiff, black beard, a red baize shirt and blue trousers, carelessly put on, and with the dirt of a week's wear in the sun and soil, with upraised hand and forefinger rigidly extended, speaking rapidly, I could easily conceive of him as the terrific Mr. Potts, and certainly the most lowering-looking man I had ever seen! I am sure I should once have trembled all over at the thought of such an interview; but there he stood, tearful and yielding as a little child! There stood the father, yearning and solicitous for his son, disarmed of his turbulence and pugnacity, and ready to do anything for me and for the best welfare of his child.

"Mind ye, Miss Hudson, my word for it, Tim shall do all you want, as sure as Monday morning comes. Go on! There is a long way before ye. Go on," and he shook my hand heartily. "God bless you! You are a little creature for such things, but do your best by the boy," and he turned back, going as fast as he could towards his farm.

Now that I was alone again, my strung and suppressed feelings were indulged, and I sat down and wept with thankfulness and joy. The afternoon work, begun in trembling, and weakness, and much halting, ending thus in peace and satisfaction! I could scarcely realize it. I seemed almost to be dreaming. Had I actually bearded Tim's father in his den, and come forth unhurt?

"Oh, how much better to go through with anything!" I exclaimed to myself. "What mountains people make of mole-hills, for want of a little resolution! 'Never give up till you have done all you can do,' my mother always says; and, as for Mr. Potts, he has some kind feelings; I have found that out. I am so glad I went. Truth and justice! those are the things to bring people to terms!"

I was not far off from the spot where a few hours before I had sought heavenly aid. I now ran thither, and, again kneeling, thanked God for this peaceful termination of my doubts and difficulties, and besought him, for Christ's sake, to enable me to choose that good path which leads to Him and His blessed kingdom. Then hastily did I retrace my steps to Mr. Green's. It was late when I arrived.

"There is the mistress!" shouted one of the little Greens, espying me from the top of a wood-pile. "The mistress has come!"

Mr. Green soon appeared, and his good wife with Jerry in her arms. All came forth to meet me, or to see if the mistress had actually returned alive.

"Glad to see you," said Mr. Green, his white teeth unusually visible, for he was a grave man, seldom indulging in a smile. But he did smile now, and it was a very hearty smile too. I felt that I was welcome.

"Esther, go and see if the mistress's supper is ready!"

"Now she is gone," (for I hold that children should not know everything,) said Mr. Green, "what has come of it? Do tell! Did you see the old man? I could not help thinking of you all the afternoon;" and he folded his arms, as if to hear a very solemn account. Mrs. Green was all eyes, peeping over her good man's back.

"Yes, I saw him! He has taken my part, and is going to make Tim do all I require of him, even if he has to come to the school himself to see to the matter!" And I sat down, wearied out, on the door-step.

"Bless me! Is it possible!" said Mrs. Green.

"I never heard the like!" echoed Mr. Green.

"Supper is ready!" cried Esther.

"I see you are a good match for the old man !" said Mr. Green, eyeing me with curiosity and interest.

"Well, she has got the most of what I call real courage," said old Uncle Jerry, when it was rehearsed to him, "of any girl I ever saw."

They did not know the struggles, but only the results, and wondered and admired. These were the consequences of—never giving up. From ill health and effeminate habits, and seclusion from the excitements which stir the other sex to action, women are apt to shrink from efforts which give them trouble, or call for resolute exertion. To accomplish anything of great importance, they must be early trained to steady determination and thoughtfulness in the pursuit of duty.

It cannot be denied that there is among us too much of the education of show. The women of our age and country want that which will enable them to think and act with vigour and ability, in their proper sphere. To live, and to live right, is to toil, to struggle, to press forward amid obstacles. We have a warfare to accomplish, a victory to gain, over the world, the flesh, and the devil. Grace is promised us, and it is our part to be watchful, prayerful, and faithful unto death, when we shall receive a crown of glory, which the Lord, the righteous Judge, shall give us in that day ; and not to us only, but to all that love His appearing.

Monday morning came. I was at the school-house early, and found Tim already there ! He was crest-fallen. Taking my seat, I could see he was restless and uneasy, shuffling hither and thither; until, at length, he marched hurriedly up to the desk and handed me a paper; then he stood a little backward, with his eyes upon the ground.

I opened and read it. It was a full confession of his faults, asking forgiveness, and promising amendment.

" Father says I must read this out loud before' the school!" said Tim, in a husky voice.

The event was all I could desire. Fortified by parental authority, Tim gave me little trouble afterwards. I could forgive a few freaks in his first attempts to steady himself in the path of well-doing.

———

Left much alone, away from the peculiar sympathies and interests which filled up almost every hour while at home, much time was left on my hands for reflection. My mother's intense interest for the spiritual good of her children, and her almost agonizing desire to behold them with their affections and interest devoted to the service of their gracious Lord and Master, came forcibly home to me. Her instruction and her prayers returned upon my soul with more power than when she first uttered them in my ear.

I felt there was a great work before me. The claims of my Creator and Redeemer upon me were not to be set aside nor trifled with. The tenor of all her letters was to urge me to this service in the spring of my youth, that my best days might be given to my best Friend. In answer to a passage in one of my letters, in which I intimated that I could not change my own heart, and what then could I do? she wrote thus :—

"No, my child, you cannot, indeed, change your own heart. That is the work of the Holy Spirit; but you can break up the fallow ground, and open your heart to receive him. You can ask, seek, call, knock. That is your work, a work which you only can do, and which you must some time do, if you ever expect to find salvation. And that is the work, I pray you to begin now—NOW, before the cares and the deceitfulness of the world shall choke your heart, and render it altogether barren and unfruitful. You say you cannot help thinking of the subject, that you are sad and oppressed, and wish the burden removed. Happy is it that you feel thus, my child! God has disturbed your security, in order that you may find peace in believing. Never give up the subject until you do find it. Strive, agonize in prayer, that he would lift the veil from your eyes, so that you may behold his beauty; that you may be able to cast your burden at his feet; that by faith you may give up to him your whole heart and cordially submit to his will. This is the first step in the formation of your religious character, and of vital importance, because the FIRST.

"I trust my dear child knows what are some of the duties of a Christian life. May she soon exercise herself therein, with diligence and godly fear. Now, Jane, NOW is the only time you are sure of. Act as for your life, for is not eternal life the prize?"

I received the letter containing this paragraph, at an important moment.

The people of the district, and of the place where I worshipped, were of a denomination different from the one in which I had been edu- cated ; yet was their piety sincere and unaffected, and their minister a truly godly man. He obeyed the apostolic injunction, being instant in season and out of season, for the good of souls com- mitted to his charge. Though it was towards the harvest, when the husbandmen were most busy in their fields, and the women in their dairies, a great seriousness spread itself over a portion of his flock, and several were inquiring the way of life.

A meeting for religious conversation and in- struction had been appointed, one evening, at my little school-house. All the neighbourhood around attended, old and young, though the meeting was especially designed for the youth. Every singer, bearing a tallow candle and iron candlestick, with his tune-book, might have been seen, as the darkness gathered, issuing from lanes and paths here and there, and going in the direction of the school-house.

"Are you going, ma'am?" had asked one and another. The school-mistress evaded the ques- tion, and answered ambiguously. A conflict was going on in her bosom; the claims of God on one side, and the secret disinclination of a sinful heart on the other. She knew her duty, but was averse from it. When she heard of

the appointment, conscience instantly urged her
going, bidding her use every means in her power
to awaken and to influence her on a subject so
deeply important.

The voice of the tempter came, with curious
and artful insinuations.

"These people are not your people," he said.
"They want to proselyte you."

"You are the school-mistress, and everybody
will be watching you and talking about it."

"There is time enough ; no haste is necessary.
Wait for a more convenient season. You can
be just as good in your own bed-room."

"What is the use of going to the meeting
to-night? You are tired."

She did not know then how good and blessed
a thing it is to meet with the people of God.
She listened to the tempter; and though good
Mr. Green entreated, "Do go with us to the
house of prayer!" and looked grieved as she
coldly answered "No," she saw him and uncle
Jerry and Mary hasten down the road, leaving
her in no enviable frame of mind.

Ah! no, I was ill at ease. No sooner had
their forms faded away in the twilight, than I
flew to my bed-room, and buttoned the door.
Sitting down by the open window, I looked out
upon the fields, and trees, and skies, dimly dis-
cerned, but not less suggestive of grave and
solemn thoughts of God. Even the deep and
mysterious hum of insects reminded me of the
presence of God. A sense of his omniscience
and omnipotence came over me, and his eye
seemed to be searching my inmost soul. I felt

that I could not bear the inspection. I wanted, like one of old, to go away and hide myself. I was guilty and vile in his sight, and felt an abhorrence of myself.

What should I do? What *could* I do? I wanted to be released from the bondage of sin. I longed for the peace and light and strength which a believing knowledge of Christ Jesus could alone impart, and yet I knew not how to get it. I was groping darkly about. Was it not then my duty to seize hold of any means that could shed light upon my difficulties? Should I not put myself in the attitude to receive instruction? Had not the Father of my spirit opened to me a way to receive the instruction I then needed, at the little school-house, that very evening? Had I not turned my back proudly upon it? What would my mother say? Oh that she were near, to guide and counsel me! Turn which way I would, I was wretched. I could not pray. I hated to think. I flung myself on the bed in a forced indifference, nor did I move or stir, or know how time passed, until the strain,

"Rock of ages, cleft for me !"

in a well-known tune, oftentimes sung at home, broke upon my ear from the kitchen. It was Mr. Green. There seemed a peculiar sweetness in the singing, as if it gushed joyfully from the heart. I repeated aloud the first two lines, and tried to feel them. I recited the entire hymn, turning portions of it into prayer.

It was a night of conflict, and the dawn was not yet.

H 3

My mother's letter came two days afterwards. It was not calculated to allay my apprehensions, or quiet my conscience. The more I reflected, the more important appeared immediate decision upon the subject. I felt that it must not be put off; but my views were dark and clouded. I wanted the instruction which Christian experience could alone give me. Where was it to be obtained? I had neglected it when an opportunity offered directly suited to my case, and now what was to be done?

"Do something! Do not give up!" I seemed to hear my mother say, again and again.

The sabbath came, but gave me little relief. On Monday, one of my scholars came up to me, and after some embarrassment and hesitation said, "Ma'am, the minister is going to have a meeting at grandmother's to-night. Mother wants to know if you would not like to come?"

I looked up at the child.

"Yes, I will come, Margaret," I answered, quickly.

Ought I not, in a time like that, to avail myself of every opportunity to be instructed? My conscience responded, Yes. Many a soul has been lost, for want of promptness and decision at the right moment—at the time when God's Spirit is awakening the conscience; when the motives and claims of the gospel are (by Divine grace) seen in something of their true light, and when the importance of choosing THIS DAY whom we will serve, comes upon us like an awful reality. It is dangerous to trifle at such a time. The example of Felix is for our warning.

"Yes, I must go," I thought; "I want more instruction, and I must use every means in my power to get it. I must do it now."

Margaret's grandmother's house was distant, and the night was dark. I could take a lantern. Then I thought of asking Mr. Green to accompany me; it would afford me an opportunity of speaking to him upon the great subject agitating my heart. But the difficulty was in asking him. How long I stood with my hand on the latch, doubting, deliberating, ashamed to ask him, and yet afraid not to ask him!

"Go forward!" said something within me.

Then I went out towards the barn to find him, but he was not to be seen, and I was near giving up again, and returning into the house. But, passing by the woodpile, there was Mr. Green, fixing a saw. My request was made.

"I will go, and be thankful to go," answered the good man.

At the appointed hour, we went together to Margaret's grandmother's house. That evening I shall never forget—that dark, warm evening in August. It was the starting point of my religious history. A detail of all that occurred I need not give. Suffice it to say, that I was amply rewarded for the step which I had taken.

Mr. Green's conversation resolved most of my doubts, and cleared up many perplexities. As we went along, I felt that I could speak to him unreservedly, and from him I received all the needed guidance which it was my object to secure at the grandmother's. Though a humble and unlearned man, he was "mighty in the Scriptures," and clear in his religious experience; and he, among many others, was a striking example of what the Bible can do for a man, intellectually as well as morally. His tone of thought and conversation was striking and elevated—the result, not of education, but of a deep and constant study of his Bible. I sometimes think I have never met one since, whose teaching to a young inquirer was more clear and convincing, more pungent and direct. The weeks spent beneath his roof were in a truly refined and Christian atmosphere; his prayers were as if he met his Maker face to face; his daily life like one intimate with Christ. Mr. Green has long since been numbered with the dead. The world is better for his having lived in it.

Many, many times have I thanked God for the decision of that night. If promptness and resolution are needed in the business of life, just as much, if not more, are they needed in business pertaining to the concerns of the soul. Now I felt the value of my mother's training. She had taught me the importance of doing, and doing myself, and even in this matter I was unable to get away from the force of her reasonings and old habits formed beneath her eye. It is frequently hard to act, and act for and by one's self; but the indecision and tardiness of action, which often render right conclusions and fine principles good for nothing, really bring a thousand more snares and obstacles and evils around your path, and harass your mind a thousand fold more, than a straightforward, resolute pursuit of duty will ever do. Try it, and see.

According to the engagement with Mr. Sykes, I was teaching twelve weeks, and received six pounds. When the three months expired, several families desired me to remain six weeks longer, and keep a private school, for which they allowed me five shillings a week and my board. It was a very small school, but a very pleasant one.

At the close of my whole residence in the district, my earnings amounted to twenty-four dollars. Seven pounds ten shillings! I had never seen, much less had I ever handled, so large a sum; and it was mine, fairly and honestly mine! I felt amply repaid for every hot day's toil in the little, black, sunny school-house.

It would carry me through six months' board at D——. If money is valuable in proportion to what it can accomplish for us, how great was the value of this sum to me!

On a bright September morning, in the golden season of harvest, Elisha Sykes drove up, in his green wagon, to take me home again. I did not then know all the good I had gained in that summer among the woods. I did not then know how much richer I went back to my mother, in good things more substantial and enduring than money. At no period was I more thoroughly educating myself for the great duties of maturer life. The arms and equipments and furnishing, given me at home, were then tested, to see how useful they were in fitting me for the duties and emergencies of every-day duty. I was at work, and there is nothing like working to enable us to find our true position in the world.

As I rode by the school-house, there was a sorrowful and yet joyful farewell in the last look I gave it. The last! I have never seen it since.

AT SCHOOL.

NEVER was money husbanded like mine. Though my brown hood was very brown, and the sleeves of my Scotch plaid pelisse extremely short, notwithstanding the eking out of a cuff, and the application of an old strip of chinchilla, they were to be worn another winter. To buy new clothes was not to be thought of. There must be no breaking in upon the treasured sum. During the winter, my mother gave me what I could earn with my needle, to supply me with new spring clothes and suitable books for study.

As spring advanced, I looked forward with animation to school pursuits. But there were important preliminaries to settle. Could I board for five shillings a week, as Sarah May said could be done at a mile's walk from the school? Cornelia doubted it; she gave ten shillings. And then the tuition. Could I get a place upon the charity fund? Mr. Hale promised my mother to intercede for me, but he had left town without thinking of it, not to return for many weeks.

"After all, Jane," she said, beholding my anxiety, "it is better, if possible, to do all you can yourself. Other people's hands are full, and we must not expect too much from them. Write yourself to Mrs. B——, and ascertain what you can depend upon; tell her exactly your circumstances."

"You write, mother!"

She looked at me and smiled.

"Nay, my dear," said she, "I want you to learn to do such things. Write to Mrs. B——, say just what your situation is, and what you want at her school. Write as if you were talking to me—briefly and simply. I will read your letter, and see if it answers the purpose."

Thus encouraged, I sat down to try. It was a day or two before I was satisfied with the production; nor was I then, but my mother should see it. With two additions and a subtraction, she thought it would do. I carried the letter and put it in the office with deeper solicitude, but more calmness, than characterized the proceedings of the Green Lane note. Indeed, I was growing business-like, "learning to labour and to wait." It was not many days—it was even before an answer was expected—that George bounded into the house with a letter in his hands.

"That is what I like," exclaimed he. "Now Jane will not have to wait, wait, wait, every day. She is a business woman, mother, you may depend upon it."

"Mother, you open it!" I said, tremblingly.

"No, my child, calm yourself, and read it to us," she said, passing it from George.

On breaking the seal, I stood and paused a moment.

"Is it a good or bad omen, coming so soon, George?"

"Good, good! Think everything is good until you know to the contrary. Come, dash into it, Jane," he exclaimed, brightly.

"George has the true philosophy," said my mother.

The letter was opened and read, proving highly satisfactory to the group most interested in its contents. Board could be obtained for five shillings, and, if willing, I could earn my tuition in some work pertaining to the buildings of the institution.

"There is nothing like trying, mother, is there?" I cried, joyfully. "Then I am really going to D——, really going!"

Though my preparations were simple enough, yet the event was so great that it seemed like fitting out an expedition to California.

Cornelia seemed glad when I communicated the delightful fact to her, but less glad than I expected; and less glad, perhaps, than she would have been two years before.

"Oh, you will be so far behind us all!" she said. "If you had only gone in the first place, you could have 'finished' with us this summer or next!"

"But you know I could not go then."

"I do not see why you could not as well as now," she answered, carelessly. And indeed

Cornelia could never be persuaded that whatever was wanted might not be done as well at
one time as another. Her wishes were gratified,
and she could see no reason why others' should
not be. There are many Cornelias in the
world.

Again the season of departure arrived, and
our village sent its spring delegation to the
school at D——: Cornelia, the Mays, and two
other girls and myself. It was a dull, rainy
day, a day that saddened the departure of some
of us, even to tears; but I was buoyed up to
womanly firmness by a keen relish for the
duties before me, and of their importance, con-
sequent upon the exertions already made to
attain them.

New faces, new duties, new interests, new
associations, were before me.

SCHOOL DAYS.

STUDIES, a long walk to and from school,
the care of some of the academy rooms, so fully
occupied my time, that I saw little of my old
companions. Indeed, there was little time to
think of any thing but our regular succession
of duties. So systematic was every arrangement, so prompt was every teacher, that any
remissness or procrastination on the part of a
pupil was immediately noticed and marked;
and so strong was popular opinion on the side
of good order, that no one, possessing any self-
respect, ever wished to come under censure in

these points.   There was an earnestness and
promptitude in obeying the requirements of
school which I had never before seen, and
which I now think had an important bearing
in the formation of character in those under Miss
——'s care.   Sometimes I was grieved, that a
stranger in school as I was, since the first day,
neither Cornelia nor the Mays seemed to take
notice of me.   True, there were a hundred and
twenty scholars, and we were in different classes.
How then could we see much of each other?

Three weeks passed, and, behold, a letter from
my mother and George and Mary!   A delightful
home letter, full of news and good advice!   It
was with some difficulty that I could steady my
mind for the next recitation.

I longed to tell Cornelia, and repeat to her
several little particulars of the village news.
When school closed, she was not to be found.
While the girls were dispersing I read it over
again, and never letter seemed so interesting.   I
was in the midst of sweeping the large school-
room, when, with two or three others coming
down stairs, I saw Cornelia, hanging on the arm
of one whom the girls called " the heiress."

" Oh, Cornelia," I cried, throwing down the
broom, " I have a letter from home!"

" Indeed!" she answered, coldly, passing on.

" What did that girl tell it to you for?"
asked her companion, haughtily.   " Oh, this
shocking dust!"

" Poor thing!   I suppose she takes a fancy
to me," whispered Cornelia, in a low tone, but
not so low that it did not reach my ear.   They
went out at the door.

The difference in our position flashed upon me!

For an instant I was indignant. Then, wounded and disappointed, I sat down upon a bench; then kicked away the broom with my foot. My right hand went into my pocket, clasping the letter.

" She, who knows me so well! She —— " I strove to feel right. My eye fell on the neglected broom. " She may look down upon me; but after all, what matters it? But let me not despise my poor broom," repentant thoughts coming thick and fast, " for it is my broom that gives me my tuition, after all. I might not have been here, with all my money, if it were not for this! If the other girls do not sweep, I do, and I am glad of it. My mother says, if we expect to get any great good in this life, we must labour for it. Cornelia and I are in different situations, and I must be content to bear with the circumstances which will arise out of this difference. My mother always says I can bear it;" and, covering my eyes, I breathed a silent prayer for a meek and forgiving spirit. Again reading over that portion of the letter written by my mother, I arose to finish the work.

This incident was a key to some other mysterious signs of coolness, which I did not before understand, in Cornelia's manner. But it did not depress nor discourage me, and I could forgive it; but I could not so easily forget it. It hung like a cobweb about me, for many days. Cornelia and I had so often played together, and once we used to sit side by side at school;

but we were children then, and had not learned
the distinctions which wealth makes, even at
school !

"Never think of slights a moment, unless
they are caused by your own misconduct," my
mother says. "It is no matter what people may
happen to think of us, provided we act our parts
well." But then it would be so pleasant to talk
over things with Cornelia! So pleasant! Ah,
well, "it is not for pleasant things alone that we
live," my mother says; "it is to do, with all our
might, what is before us to do. Our heavenly
Father gave us the work." And the subject
was soon effectually banished by a resolute ad-
herence to that work. Indeed, I was surprised
to find myself so tranquil at any remembrance
of it. After all, does not half of the unhappi-
ness of life grow out of jealousies and slights
and envyings, which a hearty and resolute attention to the work before us (and everybody
has a work to do, whether he thinks so or not)
would put to flight, and spread a blue sky over
the heart.

———

Having been placed in classes somewhat more
advanced than myself, double diligence was necessary to maintain a desirable position among
my school-fellows. I began to feel hurried. An
almost feverish interest took possession of me,
urging me forward in every school-duty, while
other duties (quite as important in their place)
were apt to be carelessly discharged, or altogether neglected. Evening devotions were prone
to be put off, until drowsiness compelled me to

leave my studies, rendering me as unfit for prayer as for study. My first waking thoughts more frequently alighted upon an equation in algebra, or a difficult sum in arithmetic, than upon "mercies renewed every morning and fresh every evening." Not having yet united with the people of God, (for it was not then so common for youth to join themselves to the visible church as it is now,) I still trusted I was a child of God; and during the winter I had enjoyed great comfort in the discharge of religious duty, and from the conversations and prayer of my mother. For several weeks, all the importance of punctuality in private devotion was deeply felt. My mother's letters often warned me against the temptation of setting it aside, or crowding it away from its proper season, by other occupations and interests. By and by, I began to read my Bible less seriously; then, perhaps, a verse or two, with the mind so much upon other things, that I could scarcely tell their import. Then followed hasty and wandering prayer, with thoughts running hither and thither. I could not fix them. I could not feel what I needed nor what I asked. Then the hasty arrangement of my chamber— "I will sweep to-morrow," or, "I will dust it to-morrow." Books were in disorder. I could find neither comb nor pocket-handkerchief. Nothing was in place, and consequently nothing at hand. I spent much time, when every moment was precious, in seeking about for the commonest article; and this was to me more annoying and perplexing, because at home every thing was perfectly regulated, and we had been trained to have a place for every thing, and, what is more difficult, to keep every thing in its place.

"It will save so much time," my mother used to say, "and economy of time is quite as important as economy of money."

The consequence was, I was in a perpetual hurry, worried and irritated, and astonished and ashamed of my irritation. There was a weight upon my spirits, and I could not feel any cheerful alacrity in any thing, not even in my studies.

One Wednesday morning I awoke suddenly, with the impression that I had overslept myself. Jumping quickly up, and seizing my book, I sat down at an open window facing the east, where the morning had dawned sufficiently to see to read. Not half awake, I strove to study. I read the page over and over again, yet it did not appear to convey any meaning. I could get no hold of it. I could not remember it.

"But I must stick to it."

Half-dressed, uncombed and unwashed, there I sat. The breakfast bell startled me.

"Half-past six, and nothing accomplished!" I cried, in despair, looking at myself, my bed, my books, and my room, and the little pocket Bible on the floor under the table. Never had my room exhibited a spectacle like that! My conscience reproached me. When would every thing be in order again? All the good habits which I had been violating came up to shame me. What would my mother say?

I think I never looked around so bewildered

and mortified, though alone, and none near me to reprove. Making a hasty toilet, I went to a late breakfast, and then how little time to finish what was before me, and be ready for school at half-past eight.

"All this comes from giving undue time and attention to one duty at the expense of others," I said, bitterly, on again surveying my dis-ordered apartment. "How much mother used to caution us against it; but I am sure I never realized it until now."

What was to be done first? I took up my Bible and tried to read, but where was the quiet of mind necessary to a due reflection upon what I read? I could not stop.

Then a tramping of feet upon the stairs, and two or three knocks at the door.

"Oh, the girls!" I exclaimed, testily, running to hide this thing and that.

Opening the door, they cried, "Have you decided to go upon the expedition this after-noon? Do, Jane, decide to go! We have walked over here on purpose to persuade you;" and their happy, bright faces glowed with ani-mation.

"Oh, it is almost time for school! I suppose you overslept yourself!" exclaimed one, gazing good-humouredly around. I was in no mood to hear any thing.

"No, I am not going this afternoon. I thought the girls understood me so. It costs more than I can afford, and I am not going," I answered, standing with my hand on the latch, and never asking them to sit down.

"Oh, we shall have such a good time! and,

dear Jane, you look this minute as if you needed a ride," affectionately putting her arm around me. At any other time her kindness would have been pleasant; but as it was, I shrank away, saying, " Indeed I cannot go! You can all afford it, I cannot!"

The girls soon left, and then how my incivility troubled me!

" Oh!" I sighed, in an ocean of trouble.

The forenoon passed. Hard pushed and restless, I made total failures in two recitations— the first I had made! and I was wretched enough.

While at dinner, a little note was handed me, from a boy at the door. It contained an invitation from some of my class-mates to accompany them upon the afternoon ride to a beautiful pond ten or twelve miles distant, signed by her who had so affectionately urged my going in the morning.

The different classes, under the care of a teacher, not unfrequently used to club together and hire a stage-coach to ride out to some of the delightful places around, and spend the afternoon. The present was such an occasion. Their kindness, so undeserved, touched my heart.

" Go! certainly go! It will do you a world of good," urged Mrs. Bond.

" I will go to get away from myself!" I cried, inwardly. An acceptance was sent. Then I ran up stairs to hasten preparations.

" Clean stockings! Clean stockings!" I hunted around after a pair of clean stockings.

One pair! unmended. Another pair!—Another pair! both unmended. Alas, should it be confessed?

I cowered before those unmended stockings, with shame and sorrow. I blushed, in their presence, at what my mother would have considered an unpardonable neglect. I felt that I had lost ground; that I was far, far behind my plain duty.

"What! is not this too bad! Holes at both elbows, as well as holes in both stockings!" I exclaimed, bitterly, sinking down into a seat, and covering my face with both hands. How long I sat I know not; but I arose, and finding paper and pencil, wrote a note, at the risk of being considered fickle, or any thing else which the girls chose to consider me. My mind was made up not to go. "I see how it is," thinking as I went about my chamber; "in the ardent pursuit of one thing, every thing else has been neglected. I have broken link after link in the chain of duty, and what disorder comes of it! What crowding, and trouble, and perplexity!" And I am sure I never realized before what sore disadvantages arise from pushing one duty out of its appropriate place. At home we had always done every thing in its time, and the consequence was, there was time for every thing.

"I must stop now and resolutely examine my chamber. I will not fly away from its evils, for then I must only come home and meet them again, and not a jot will be gained. Matters would be worse by to-morrow. I must stop, and never give up until they are righted once more—until I retrace all my hurried steps, and start where I was a week ago."

"It is a beautiful afternoon," I said, as the summer wind came softly into the window, where I lingered a moment, and where I soon espied the coach driving towards the house, notwithstanding the note.

"You do not often get a chance to ride! Go! It is a sign you ought to go, that the coach is coming in spite of your note! Go!" So said temptation.

"No! No! No! It is but a small matter whether I enjoy an afternoon's ride or not; but it is a very great matter whether, when I find things going wrong, I have resolution and firmness enough to stop and look at them, and try to get right again. 'Never fly from perplexities,' my mother says. 'Meet them and thread your way through them, like a true woman.'"

"Your troubles do not amount to much, after all! Little affairs, just in your chamber. Nobody knows it, or will think the less of you. Go! Have a good time. 'It will be the same a hundred years hence! Go!" continued temptation; while the carriage stopped, and several voices cried joyfully,

"Come, come! Jane Hudson, I am so glad you are going Be quick! We shall have such a fine time!" So they all exclaimed, even before I could reaffirm the decision of the note.

"Nonsense!" they cried. "You can go just as well as not. Besides, Miss B—— says you look as if you needed a ride. She wants you to go! Come, come!"

I shook my head and left the window. Mrs. Bond ran up stairs to see into the matter.

"Not going!" she exclaimed. "My dear Miss Hudson, you will study yourself to death. You have looked so pale for a week."

I begged that she would suffer me to decide according to my own judgment, and to assure the girls that, although I thanked them for their kindness, and under other circumstances might have enjoyed the ride, yet, as it was, I could not go.

"It is not hard study that makes me pale," I said, as Mrs. Bond departed; "for I have exercise enough. It is for the want of a serene and tranquil mind," fastening the door after her. "Perhaps these are little matters, all in my own chamber—perhaps they are—but then they are the matters which help to discover and to form our characters, and so are all-important to us. My mother says there is a right and there is a wrong, and I am sure it can never be the same to go right and to go wrong." I looked wistfully at the departing carriage on that beautiful summer afternoon, but I remained firm to my resolution.

Sometimes I have considered this as one among the most important decisions of my life.

The time and attention of woman, in her proper sphere, the home-sphere, are necessarily employed upon a great multitude of humble duties and little obligations—little, I mean, apart, yet vast in the aggregate, but which are the more apt to get deranged on this very account. Hence it is to be feared they too often and too easily get out of place. Undone or ill-done duties, accumulating upon her hands, produce confusion and vexation in her whole household. Who has not seen wives, and daughters, and mothers perplexed, and anxious, and half sinking on this account, and knowing scarcely why or how all these difficulties arise? Let the courage and firmness exercised in other matters come to her aid here. Do not attempt to fly from them. Do not imagine matters will go smoothly by and by, without any effort on your part to produce it. It is not so. True, you may at length settle down in the conclusion to let things take their course; but you will be neither comfortable nor happy yourself, nor will you make comfortable or happy those around you. You must stop and know what link or links you have lost in the chain. You must face the results of neglected duty; firmly and patiently retrace your steps, and set things right again. Give yourself no rest, and suffer yourself to engage in no pleasure, until they are righted. While it is unquestionably best never to go wrong, it is unquestionably better to stop when you fear you are wrong, and apply an immediate remedy to the evils about you, than suffer them to accumulate. How many household disorders might be checked in the beginning, in this way, and tranquillity restored!

It must be confessed the afternoon was not a very happy one, at least no further happy than in the hope of getting in the right track again.

How busy I was! Trunk, drawers and table were thoroughly ransacked and put in order,— all my books and work rearranged.

"Holes at both elbows!" I inwardly ejaculated every now and then. Holes at both elbows, indeed! I may be a very good scholar, but what does that signify if I do not take care of my clothes, and keep my chamber with neatness and propriety! Good scholarship cannot sew, or sweep, or patch, or cook, or keep home in good order. These are among my appropriate duties, come what will, my mother says, and these it would be a shame for me to neglect! My main business now is study, I know, but not to the slighting of a single other daily duty. "There is time for every thing," my mother always said.

But while our chamber neglects can be repaired, it is not so easy to make up for the neglect of closet duties. My experience of this was bitter, and I can feelingly counsel others to beware, above all things, how they trifle with their religious habits. There are great temptations surrounding the path of the godly student, whether girl or boy, even in the retirement of the chamber; and they are the greater, because they steal over us unawares, and are not accounted temptations. In the ardent pursuit of knowledge, (a pursuit in itself excellent and desirable,) absorbing the time not unfrequently from early morning till late at night, the hour for private devotion is oftentimes imperceptibly encroached upon, or attended to with thoughts and affections too jaded and too preoccupied to receive much benefit from them. Thus it may

K

go on, day after day, and week after week, the student all the while less watchful of himself, because he feels himself safe in the seclusion of his study, apart from the ordinary temptations of the world, until he at last finds himself growing irritable and anxious, pressed by a heavy weight upon his spirits, destitute of the light and warmth which a genuine religious experience always gives to the soul; with little relish for his Bible and for prayer, and wandering far, very far from his Saviour. Mournful state! Do you now fly to your studies, with increasing avidity, for refuge and comfort? Alas, you will find that they cannot give you the peace for which you sigh, and you wonder why they perplex and harass you more than formerly—why you are dispirited and pushed as for your life. You wonder why the zest is gone.

To every school-girl, then, who is trying to live in obedience to her Saviour, and who hopes she has taken the first steps in a religious life, let me address a caution. Beware of suffering your studies to encroach upon the hour allotted to reading your Bible, to reflection, and to prayer. Do not wait until you are asleep over your algebra, before you put it aside and take up your Bible. Do not hurry carelessly over your morning prayer, lest there should not be time enough for your philosophy. There is time enough for every thing necessary to be done. There must be time for you to seek the favour and forgiveness of your heavenly Father. Depend upon it, all the firmness and punctuality so necessary for the exercise of the school-room, and for the suitable arrangements of your chamber, are at least just as necessary in your strictly religious duties. You can never study to the best advantage, until your mind has been tranquillized and invigorated by earnest and believing prayer. You are never so well pre-pared for vigorous progress, as when living habitually under the truth, "Thou God seest me." Try it and see. Strive early every morn-ing to impress upon your mind, and ask God to impress by his Spirit, the great truth con-tained in those four little words, "Thou God seest me." Believe me, it will give you a quiet though unconquerable energy in the discharge of every duty, such as no motives drawn from this life can give you. The time spent in con-templating it is not lost. You will study all the better for it. It will make you less dis-tracted and anxious. It will make you more steady, true, and calm. And so of any great religious truth. Every morning, clear and prepare your mind for the day's duty, by reflec-tions like these. You will need it for the growth of your Christian character, especially while occupied as much as you are by the study of physical truths.

If you find that you are losing ground in your religious hopes and enjoyments, that your habits to-day are not so exemplary as they were two days, or a week, or two weeks, or months ago, STOP, just where you are ! STOP, and ask why it is so? STOP, and, if possible, retrace your steps. STOP, and get right again. Humble and repentant, go again to Jesus. It will, perhaps, be painful and difficult, but let every

young Christian do it; patiently, firmly, and
with a whole heart, do it, remembering always
that life has failed of its great purpose, if it is
not animated by that holy energy which springs
from a loving faith in the truths of the gospel.

The next day witnessed me in the retirement
of my chamber, and when I again went forth,
it was with an experience never to be forgotten.

———

In two years I left school, in the same class
with Cornelia Gordon and the Mays.

I will not say that I then "finished my
education," for it was rather laying a deep and
firm foundation for future improvement.

Miss B—— made friendly inquiries into my
real circumstances, which being fieely disclosed
to her, she had offered her aid in meeting the
expenses of my second year at school.

Soon after leaving D——, an eligible situation
as teacher quickly offered, through the kind
recommendation of Miss B——, which, in a
short time, enabled me to repay her timely
assistance.   Nor was it long before I enjoyed
the privilege of sending Mary through the same
course of study with this excellent friend, at the
same institution.

My mother and Jemmy hardly knew how they
could spare her, so bright and lively was she,
and never away from home.   But my mother
needed her less than she formerly did, and
could well spare her awhile, for we (George
and I) were ever dropping something into my
mother's purse, so that she never uses her

needle now, save as the "maker and mender" for her own household.

And the dear old homestead! It is the dear old homestead always, and we shall always love it and cherish it as the spot where we passed a happy and industrious childhood, presided over by a mother to whose judicious management we feel that we owe all our present success and usefulness.

"Such a mother!" George says; "always putting us on our own hook, and, what is so difficult, making us hang on it!"

George is a young man now, a partner with his old master, and doing well, we may conclude, from the improvements he has wrought in the homestead.

I will not say how long it is since I left the school at D——, but it is long enough to see the summing up of many lives, and the results of different principles carried out into action. In some respects they are important results.

The daily current of village news would often bring them up to view.

———

"Poor Mrs. Smith, how much she is to be pitied!"

"And those children, poor things, how they must be neglected!"

"I do not know what will become of her!"

"Do you know she is very nervous? the most trifling things trouble her."

"Why, I am told she sits from morning till

night in her rocking-chair. I should not think she let any thing trouble her much."

" Property enough! Yes, to live very comfortably upon. At least, any one but she could. She! She is so inefficient!"

" And inexperienced!"

" And indolent! Why does she not arouse herself and give her mind to her family? She has enough to occupy her."

" Why, remember how she was brought up, poor thing!"

" Well, I always said so!"

" Only think of Mrs. Smith's coming back!"

" Mrs. Smith come back!"

" Yes, a widow with four little children, but with sufficient to maintain them, if only husbanded with care and economy."

But who is Mrs. Smith?

I felt deeply interested in all I could glean of her, for she was no other than Cornelia Gordon. I had not seen her since her marriage, when she went away, with the world bright before her. Several changes had passed over her family since then.

Her father was no longer a rich man. Two older sons had managed, or mismanaged, to deprive him of the largest portion of his property. His wife was dead, and he had lived alone, a solitary old man, until the death of Cornelia's husband, when she came (with her four little ones, and a remnant of what was accounted a good fortune) to live with him.

Soon she sent a message for me to come and see her. I always loved Cornelia. Whether it was her good nature, or her prettiness, or the nice things her mother used to bestow upon us from her back door, when I used to gallop home with Cornelia; or whatever may have been the cause, I had always felt some secret drawing of the heart towards her, and long after we had made new homes far distant from each other, no early friend was so soon inquired for as Cornelia Gordon. Her present situation grieved me, and I gladly went to see her.

"Come often, very often, while you are in town," she said, on parting at our first interview, "for I have a great many things to say to you. I am quite desolate. Run in whenever you go by. I am sure it will do me good. Oh, Jane, I am not fitted for such changes as these!"

I thought her afflictions had improved her character—improved it more than could have been expected, and I willingly availed myself of her invitation to go often to see her. Indeed it was a source of secret satisfaction to me to perceive (as I thought I did) that she could rise superior to her situation, in spite of the deficiencies of her early domestic education, and enter upon the duties before her, with firmness and energy.

"I fear Cornelia will never be able to do it," said my mother, who looked too comfortable and happy, knitting away in her snug armchair, to venture an uncharitable remark about anybody. "Afflictions, necessity, repentance, good resolutions, can do much for us, even when we are old; but they can never supply entirely that kind and degree of moral hardihood, so important for the emergencies of life, which must be acquired, if acquired at all, in the season and through the incidents of youth. It must grow with our growth, and strengthen with our strength. You will always find, my child, that those make the strong characters who have borne the yoke of discipline in their youth."

While all our mother said might be true, as a general rule, I secretly felt that Cornelia's case might be an exception.

Not many days after, I went in to sit awhile with her, one afternoon.

She was sitting in her rocking-chair, with a book in her hand, and traces of tears on her cheeks.

" You would not approve of this, I am sure," reaching one hand cordially out to me, and secreting the book behind her with the other. " But I read such books sometimes to make me forget my troubles. I have a world to think about and to do! I am perplexed, sometimes, beyond measure ! " Some cloth lay uncut before her, with an old frock of little George's, and patterns and scissors.

" I feel that I ought to cut out some of the children's clothes," she said, taking up the cloth, " for economy's sake ; but, dear Jane, I have no knack at it ; I have no knack at any such things ! "

" Patience and attention are sometimes better than a knack," I said, cheerfully.

" No, no ! " and she shook her head despondingly. " I do not think so. I have been dreading this work until the poor child actually suffers for it. It is not in me to cut out."

"Nonsense, Cornelia, it is in anybody, with good hands, good sense, and good scissors! What is in the way?"

We examined together the old work, and then some new patterns. Then called George in and tried his old jacket on, discovering where it needed a little taking in here and a little letting out there. And then it was not so very long before we called in George again to fit his new one on.

"Why, it fits admirably!" cried the mother. "Oh, if I only had your knack! You had it of old, Jane."

"No knack at all, Cornelia! We can do any thing if we try. Have more confidence in yourself, Cornelia. We can do all that is allotted to us here;" and away bounded little George again.

"Ah, no," she said, despondingly, the tears coming into her eyes, "I have every day to leave so much undone that ought to be done. I am borne down with care."

"You have good help?"

"Pretty good. But," speaking more unreservedly than she had ever done before, "but father thinks I ought to try and get on with only one person. You know I have no taste for housekeeping. There is so much to see to, so much to think of, so much that is perplexing and disagreeable in the kitchen——"

"And then, on the other hand, so much that may be clean and comfortable and tasty in the kitchen," I said, in a lively tone.

She smiled languidly.

"Ah, no, it is all a task!" and then folding

her arms before her, she threw herself back in
the chair, and began to rock.

"Come, Cornelia, let us finish George's jacket.
If you will give me needle and thimble, we will
sew together awhile. Do you know there is
nothing banishes care and trouble like work?"
I tried to speak cheerfully.

"Work! work! No, I do not believe it. There
is such a thing as too much work, perpetual
work, an endless doing!" and she rocked away
very resolutely: "and, Jane, I really do not
feel adequate to all these cares."

"Your health is good, Cornelia——"

"Yes, pretty good—only a sinking and de-
pression of spirits. The noise of the children is
an excessive annoyance! I cannot bear it. I
must hire a girl to keep them amused and out
of the way,"—still rocking. "Indeed, every
day I feel more and more my own inadequate-
ness."

"You must arouse yourself, dear Cornelia.
You must feel that you *are* adequate. I do
not believe our heavenly Father ever lays more
upon us than we can bear, nor more than
is good for us, nor more than is necessary to
call forth our capabilities. We naturally are
so prone to shrink back, that we need to be
compelled to exertion."

"It is all fine, very fine," answered my companion, languidly, "it sounds beautifully. Mr.
Smith used to talk in the same style. I have
heard it all before. Sometimes I used to try
and act upon it. Sometimes I would try and
feel that burdens were not burdensome after all.
But, Jane, it is of no use. I can, for an hour,

or half a day, perhaps, hear all the children have to say, bind up sore fingers, darn old elbows, and hunt up new shoe-strings ; perhaps make a loaf of bread, or sweep the parlours.   But then remember the thousand-and-one things to be done in the house, not done, ill-done, half-done, or, perhaps entirely forgotten until Saturday night, or Sunday morning, or Monday forenoon, when children and servants huddle up to me, asking for this and for that ; and how, and why, and when is all this to be done ?   It crazes me— puts me out.   I shut myself up in my chamber, sink into my arm-chair, and try to turn off my cares awhile with a page or two of——

"But no matter, you would not approve of it. This is just myself, Jane, and I never draw my picture to any one else but you.   A deplorable picture, you will think—I know you will—for a mother and a housekeeper ; a widow, too, with a double burden.   But it is just so ; and now, what upon earth shall I do ?   I cannot, for my life, feel the cordial love for work which you talk of !   No, no ! It is not in me. The Ethiopian, you know.— Last summer, when ill, and my recovery was doubtful, I felt no dread of death.   I looked forward to it as a release. There is rest, you know, beyond the grave."

" Rest, Cornelia, for the people of God ! Rest for those who have striven, wrestled, fought the good fight, and are faithful unto death. But the fearful and unbelieving are destined to a far different state !"

Alas! all I said then, or said afterwards, produced little or no impression upon poor Mrs. Smith.   My visits were frequent, praying from the heart that she might be aroused to proper effort, both for the sake of her children and of herself. It availed nothing. The Ethiopian cannot change his skin, nor can the leopard his spots.

The habits we form in youth, abide. If we are taught to be earnest, intent, courageous, and faithful in the duties and amid the trials of youth, nothing in after years can wrest our habits from us. We must carry them with us, and, with the Divine blessing, they will fit us for its scenes and emergencies, no matter what they may be, whether of trial or prosperity.

My young friend! whose eye is passing over these pages, if you are suffered to languish away the spring of your life in self-indulgence, in shrinking and shirking from every thing that is disagreeable—in doing only what is pleasant —in a sprightly indolence or an undisciplined activity, from the effects of it upon your physical, moral, and social nature, you can never recover to the latest day of your life. Be assured of it. When you realize and begin to feel their sad influences upon you, you can do much by a vigorous process of self-improvement. The grace of God can do much for you, but you can never recover the forming period of your life. The grace of God can only be received into such a moral habitation as you have prepared for it. Its power changes your affections, and makes a new creature of you, but the habits of childhood and youth will still show themselves, and be most important helps or hindrances in all the walks of life.

Poor Mrs. Smith lived on, in indolent inefficiency, excusing herself from every duty which seemed formidable or disagreeable; and her own weakness made them appear doubly so, by the declaration that she had "no knack," "no taste," "no tact;" or "she was so situated," or "she was so unaccustomed," or "she was so inadequate." Heavily did she bear the burden of life, complaining of its crosses, appalled by its toils, and sinking beneath its perplexities. She died not long after—I might almost say, for lack of courage to live.

Ah, we must be trained to the right use of life—trained in thorough, practical, enduring habits while we are young, in order wisely and skilfully to discharge life's duties in riper years. And while this may be seen and readily acknowledged in every thing relating to our outward life, the same training is no less important for the vigorous growth of our religious character.

Notwithstanding the general prevalence of religious profession among us, the maintenance of firm and undeviating religious principles was never more difficult. Amusements called harmless, temptations most insinuating, an easy morality, fashion, a general taste for impure or at least dangerous fiction, face us at every step with their seducing influences. It is hard to keep in the narrow way, and yet there is no other way for the Christian disciple than that strait and narrow way whereof the Lord spake. It is as strait and narrow now as ever. To walk in it, what earnestness of purpose, what resolution of will, what unfaltering exertion, what prompt obedience, what unceasing prayer, what perpetual watchfulness, what an earnest pressing forward, is at all times necessary! To attain a healthy, manly, vigorous piety, a degree of piety that will truly elevate and distinguish the character, INWROUGHT HABITS OF RESOLUTION AND PERSEVERANCE ARE ALL-IMPORTANT. Is it not so?

THE RELIGIOUS TRACT SOCIETY: INSTITUTED 1799.

ANNIE SHERWOOD;
Or, Scenes at School.
With Engravings. 16mo. 1s. cloth; 2s. half-bound morocco.

CITY COUSINS.
By the Author of " Annie Sherwood."
18mo. With Engravings. 1s. 6d. boards; 2s. 6d. half-bound morocco.

THE LIVES OF THE CÆSARS;
Or, the Juvenile Plutarch.
By CATHERINE SINCLAIR.
18mo. With Engravings. 1s. 6d. boards.

HOME LIFE.
18mo. With Engravings. 1s. 6d. cloth boards; 2s. extra boards, gilt
edges.

THE CLAIMS OF THE GOSPEL ON THE YOUNG.
By the Rev. JOEL PARRER, D.D., of Philadelphia.
18mo. 1s. boards; 2s. half-bound morocco.

GUIDE TO THE SAVIOUR, FOR THE YOUNG.
With Engravings. 18mo. 1s. cloth; 2s. half-bound morocco.

THE YOUNG BOTANISTS.
Frontispiece and Engravings. 18mo. 1s. cloth; 2s. half-bound
morocco.

ROBERT DAWSON;
Or, the Brave Spirit.

With Engravings. 18mo. 1s. 6d. boards; 2s. 6d. half-bound morocco.

SIGHTS IN ALL SEASONS.

Containing "Sights in Spring," "Sights in Summer," "Sights in Autumn," and "Sights in Winter," which are published separately.
With Engravings. 16mo square. 4s. boards.

THE EXCELLENT WOMAN,
As described in the Book of Proverbs. Chap. xxxi.

16mo square. With Twenty-four steel Engravings. 3s. extra boards, gilt.

THE GIRL'S WEEK-DAY BOOK.

With a Steel Frontispiece, and other Engravings. Royal 18mo. 4s. cloth boards, gilt edges; 6s. half-bound morocco; 7s. calf.

FEMALE EXCELLENCE;
Or, Hints for Daughters.

Designed for their Use from the Time of leaving School till their Settlement in Life. 18mo Edition, 2s. boards; 3s. half-bound, or roan, or silk. 32mo Edition, 1s. 6d. boards; 2s. half-bound, or roan, or silk.

A MOTHER'S JOURNAL, DURING THE LAST ILLNESS OF HER DAUGHTER, SARAH CHISMAN.
With a Preface by JANE TAYLOR.

1s. 4d. cloth boards; 2s. 6d. roan; 3s. 6d. calf.

LETTERS TO A DAUGHTER ON PRACTICAL SUBJECTS.
By the Rev. Dr. SPRAGUE, of Albany, America.

2s. boards; 2s. 6d. half-bound; 3s. roan, or silk; 5s. calf.

FEMALE BIOGRAPHY.

Vol. I., containing Memoirs of Mrs. Judson, Mrs. Huntingdon, Mrs. Newall, and Miss Linnard. Vol. II., containing Memoirs of Mrs. Baxter, Mrs. Walker, Mrs. Turner, Lady Glenorchy, etc. Each Volume 3s. 6d. half-bound; 5s. 6d. calf.

THE MIRACLES OF CHRIST.

With Explanatory Observations, and Illustrations from Modern Travels. Embellishments. 18mo. 1s. 6d. boards; 2s. half-bound; 2s. 6d. roan or silk; 4s. calf.

BIBLE STORIES FOR THE YOUNG.

By C. G. BARTH D.D.

Translated from the Thirtieth German Edition. Revised and Enlarged. 18mo. Old Testament, 1s. cloth. New Testament, 1s. cloth. Complete, 2s. boards. Royal Edition, on fine paper, 3s. boards.

CHRISTIAN MISSIONS;

Or, a Manual of Missionary Geography and History.

By the Rev. C. PASTOR BLUMHARDT.

Edited by the Rev. C. BARTH, D.D., of Wirtemberg.

Revised. Illustrated with Maps. In 2 vols. Each vol. 2s. 6d. boards.

EASTERN ARTS AND ANTIQUITIES.

16mo square. With steel-plate Frontispiece, and numerous Illustrations. 4s. elegantly bound in cloth, gilt edges.

ELECTRICITY;

Its Phenomena, Laws, and Results.

Square 16mo. Illustrated with numerous Engravings. 3s. 6d. elegantly bound in cloth, gilt edges.

HEAT;

Its Sources, Influences, and Results.

Square 16mo. Illustrated with numerous Engravings. 3s. 6d. elegantly bound in cloth, gilt edges.

LIGHT;

Its Properties and Effects.

Square 16mo. Illustrated with numerous Engravings. 3s. 6d. elegantly bound in cloth, gilt edges.

THE HISTORY OF INSECTS.

Square 16mo. Illustrated with numerous Engravings. 3s. 6d. elegantly bound in cloth.

SHELLS, AND THEIR INMATES.

With a Frontispiece printed in Baxter's Oil Colours. 3*s.* 6*d.* elegantly bound in cloth.

THE YOUNG TRADESMAN.

18mo, 2*s.* boards; 3*s.* half-bound.

THE YOUNG WOMEN OF THE FACTORY;

Or, Hints on their Duties and Dangers.

18mo. 1*s.* cloth.

REMARKABLE PEOPLE.

Containing, "The Arab," "The Jew," and "The Egyptian."

16mo square. With Engravings. 4*s.* 6*d.* cloth boards.

KINDNESS TO ANIMALS.

BY CHARLOTTE ELIZABETH.

With Engravings.

18mo. 1*s.* cloth; 2*s.* half-bound morocco.

THE MISSIONARY BOOK FOR THE YOUNG.

A First Book on Missions.

With Engravings.

18mo. 1*s.* cloth; 2*s.* half-bound morocco.

THE ORPHAN'S FRIEND.

32mo. 8*d.* boards; 1*s.* half-bound.

THE LIFE OF OUR BLESSED LORD AND SAVIOUR JESUS CHRIST.

18mo. With Engravings. 1*s.* 6*d.* cloth boards; 2*s.* half-bound.

THE CHRISTIAN HARP.

16mo square. With an Engraved Steel Title-page. 2*s.* extra boards.

THE SEAMAN AND HIS FAMILY;

Or, Storms and Sunshine.

18mo. With Frontispiece. 1*s.* 6*d.* boards.

CHILDREN'S TRIALS.

18mo. With Engravings. 1s. 6d. cloth boards.

WANDERINGS IN THE ISLE OF WIGHT,

By the Author of the " Old Sea Captain."
16mo square. With numerous Engravings. 2s. 6d. cloth boards.

THE HISTORY OF FRANCE.

18mo. In two volumes. Illustrated with Maps. 5s. 6d. boards ; 7s. 6d.
half-bound.

SCRIPTURE NATURAL HISTORY,

Containing a Description of Quadrupeds, Birds, Reptiles,
Amphibia, Fishes, Insects, Plants, etc., mentioned in the
Holy Scriptures.

Illustrated by numerous Engravings.
Royal 18mo. 3s. boards ; 4s. extra boards, gilt edges.

THE PEOPLE OF CHINA;

Their History, Court, Religion, Government, Manners, Customs, Literature, etc. ; to which is added, a Sketch of Pro-
testant Missions.

With a Map and Embellishments.
18mo. 3s. boards ; 4s. half-bound.

THE GREAT CHANGE.

A Treatise on Conversion.

BY GEORGE REDFORD, D.D., LL.D.

With an Introduction by the Author of " The Anxious Inquirer after Salvation."

18mo. 1s. boards; 2s. elegantly half-bound morocco.

THE REFORMATION IN EUROPE.

By the Author of " The Council of Trent."

18mo. 2s. 6d. boards; 3s. 6d. half-bound.

MY SCHOOL-BOY DAYS.

18mo. 1s. 6d. boards ; 2s. 6d. half-bound morocco.

THE APPRENTICE;

Or, Affectionate Hints to a Young Friend entering upon the Business of Life.

18mo. 1s. cloth ; 2s. half-bound morocco.

THOUGHTS AMONG FLOWERS.

With Engravings.

Royal 32mo. 1s. cloth boards; 2s. half-bound morocco.

A GUIDE TO ACQUAINTANCE WITH GOD.

By the Rev. JAMES SHERMAN.

Minister of Surrey Chapel, London.

Twenty-third Edition.

18mo. 1s. boards; 1s. 6d. half-bound.

THE SPIRIT OF POPERY.

An Exposure of its Origin, Character, and Results.

In Letters from a Father to his Children.

With numerous Embellishments.

16mo square. 4s. 6d. elegantly bound in cloth, gilt edges.

THE INDIANS OF NORTH AMERICA.

Illustrated by Engravings.

16mo square. 4s. elegantly bound in cloth, gilt edges.

KIND WORDS.

By UNCLE WILLIAM.

The two Parts in one Volume. With Engravings.

2s. boards; 3s. elegantly half-bound morocco, gilt edges.

THE USEFUL CHRISTIAN ;

A Memoir of THOMAS CRANFIELD, for about fifty years a devoted Sunday-School Teacher.

18mo. 1s. 6d. cloth boards; 2s. half-bound.

Lightning Source UK Ltd.
Milton Keynes UK
UKHW021610110119
335365UK00008B/692/P